CW00435015

Death In Green

Mitchell Island, a rare sand island off the Queensland coast, has become the focus of conflict between timber workers who want to continue to log its abundant forests and conservationists who seek to ban logging. Into this potential battleground comes Damien White, ecologist and presenter of a popular TV series, to film a documentary on the island at the invitation of Hugh Grant, head of the anti-logging campaign.

Before White arrives, there is an attempt on Grant's life, seemingly by someone in Eversleigh, the mainland town which owes its existence to logging, followed by an attack by 'Greenies' on the manager of the timber mill. Then White's scriptwriter is found drowned in suspicious circumstances.

Children's author Micky Douglas agrees to step in to complete the script but is torn between his allegiance to White, his friendship with Inspector Reeves, who is investigating the scriptwriter's death, his love for Annie Mason, also working for White, and his loyalty to his friend, journalist Duke Jordan, with whom he sets out to investigate the possibility that the warring groups are being secretly manipulated by someone with quite different plans for the island.

ANNE INFANTE

Death In Green

THE CRIME CLUB
An Imprint of HarperCollins *Publishers*

First published in Great Britain in 1992
by The Crime Club, an imprint of
HarperCollins Publishers, 77–85 Fulham Palace Road,
Hammersmith, London W6 8JB

9 8 7 6 5 4 3 2 1

Anne Infante asserts the moral right to be identified
as the author of this work.

A catalogue record for this book is
available from the British Library

ISBN 0 00 232387 7

Photoset in Linotron Baskerville by
Rowland Phototypesetting Ltd
Bury St Edmunds, Suffolk
Printed and bound in Great Britain by
HarperCollins Book Manufacturing, Glasgow

For the real Hank, who kept demanding to know what became of Annie.

With special thanks to Fred and Pam for their loving hospitality and for giving me my first experience of the unique and beautiful Fraser Island.

AUTHOR'S NOTE

While Mitchell Island is obviously a thinly disguised
Fraser Island, all the characters in my story are fictitious
and are not intended to represent any persons living
or dead.

CHAPTER 1

I'm as green as the next person. I avoid buying things in plastic—whenever I have the choice, use recycled paper, give my glass bottles and jars to the local Scout troop and clean the toilet with vinegar. No phosphates down the drain for me! And I built a slatted wooden frame for compost which all the tenants use, at the bottom of the long narrow back garden at 18 Princess Road. It may not always be easy being green, but no one told me it could be dangerous —and deadly. I found that out the hard way.

Monica Wainwright grinned at me with just a hint of sympathy, blended with concern. This surprised me because, as far as I knew, everything in my life was pretty rosy—with one exception, of course. Monica was arranging bright purple-blue jacaranda flowers in the bowl in the entrance hall and I watched her warily. Her mind wasn't on the flowers and she pussyfooted awkwardly around her news. It was unlike her not to come straight to the point.

Monica is the owner/caretaker of the six flats at 18 Princess Road, a converted red-brick Victorian house in Paddington. She also acts as den-mother, friend and confidante to us tenants. She's 40-something, capable and kind, a collector of strays. Now she pushed her blonde hair off her forehead and her blue eyes scanned my face anxiously.

'Have you seen Peta this morning?'

I stiffened. Mention of Peta Ryde always put me on my guard. Tell you why later. I shook my head.

Monica used further delaying tactics, stepping back to admire her arrangement. The delicate mauve blooms contrasted brightly with the new sunny yellow paint in the hallway, making the entrance cheerful and welcoming. Then she linked her arm in mine and led me to the door of her flat.

'Come in and have a visit. We'll—er—chat, and—ah . . .'

I followed her into No. 2 and watched her not watching me as she bustled about. Her flat was in its usual organized clutter. A place for everything and everything in its place, she says, but I'm darned if I can see how she remembers where she's put things.

She swept a pile of magazines off her comfortable old sofa. Tatty but serviceable, and solid compared with modern junk.

'Sit down, Micky. I'll make us a cuppa.'

Monica has always been a dab hand at tea and sympathy. She can break down anyone's defences with a homey cuppa, a kind, attentive ear and practical advice. My wariness increased slightly. Paradoxically, at the same time, my spirits took a tentative bound.

'Why the cryptic query about Peta?' I was ever so casual. The original Mr Cool.

She sat down beside me and poured the tea. Definitely anxious, nerves on the twitch.

'Annie's coming back,' she said gently. 'Peta got a letter this morning.'

Everything inside me jumped, but I'd already guessed, from her manner. After all, it had to happen sooner or later. But why hadn't Annie written to me and let me know? Had we drifted that far apart that she'd let me find out, third hand, through Monica? Joy and resentment fought for supremacy in my gut. I don't know who won.

'Well, that's nice,' I said, with as much coolth as I could muster. 'Did she say when?'

'Micky!' Monica looked at me severely. 'Don't you dare go all male and hiding your feelings with me! Haven't you heard from Annie at all? I'd have thought . . .'

'Yes, me too,' I said, with a failed attempt at brightness. 'I haven't heard from her for months, love. What did Peta say?'

'Something about a documentary. I was so surprised I

didn't take it in. She—she's coming back to No. 18, though, to stay with Peta. I thought you must have known and just not told me.'

'No.' I didn't bother to keep the bitterness from my voice. 'I didn't know.'

'Well! She might have told you!' Monica's distress and indignation were balm to my pride. 'That's not like Annie.'

We sipped our tea, both occupied with our own private thoughts. Monica sighed.

'Apparently Annie'll be arriving next week with a film crew. They're booked in to the Sheraton, but Annie thought she'd like to stay here with Peta. Which is how I know because Peta asked me if it would be all right.'

I forced a grin, lopsided, but it was the best I could do. I felt unpleasantly numb. 'I'll be OK. We couldn't go on for much longer without sorting things out between us, so this is probably for the best.' I leaned over and kissed Monica's cheek. 'Thanks for worrying about me, love. I'll be off now. I'll ask Peta myself what Annie says.'

Safe in my flat, I looked with unseeing eyes at Carnie, my flatmate, shocked to find my numbness giving way to a shaking anger. My teeth clenched and I stood stock still until the storm abated. The hurt began to ease at last and I poured myself a stiff brandy, my hand almost steady, and took it to the sofa. Carnie joined me, kneading her claws sharply in my leg, eyes half closed in purring ecstasy. I began to stroke her slowly in an unconscious gesture, my fingers contouring her soft warmth, as I looked through the bright spring sunshine spilling across my carpet; back across eighteen long months to the hot March morning when I'd taken Annie to the International Terminal and stood, heartsick and empty, as she boarded the Qantas flight to London to take up a too good to miss offer by the Arts Council.

'I live for a year in England, researching British folklore, with the idea of tracing our own folk roots,' she told me, holding my hand to soften the blow. 'I'll finish with a radio series.'

I was stunned. 'I didn't know you'd applied for a grant.'

It seemed she hadn't. She'd received the offer out of the blue, on the strength of a folk series she'd written and performed the previous year. She'd told me what a wonderful chance this was, a once in a lifetime opportunity, she *couldn't* say no, and it would be good for us to have some time apart. She needed to think about us before she decided whether or not to accept my proposal.

I knew better. She knew I loved her, that she was the most precious thing in my life, but she was afraid. There were times, she said, when she saw a touch of unreliability in me, a recklessness in the face of danger, a tendency to have fun and revel in trouble—her words, not mine. I tried to convince her I'd be a model husband, a reliable slippers and pipe mate, or whatever she wanted. And all the time I knew she was right. There's always been this streak of what my father calls insanity which many years ago, to his horror, caused me to throw over my hard-earned degrees and turn my back on the safe, solid world of business to write children's books. It was probably Laney's fault—my favourite relative, Great-Aunt Melanie Carter-Jones. But please don't ever call her Great-Aunt, or let on I told you. She happens to hate it and it conjures up an image of a staid, elderly lady, all twin-sets, pearls and propriety. Laney, or 'Looney Laney' to my family, is eccentric, child-like, impulsive and full of the joy and wonder of life. She was my greatest influence. I say don't blame me, but Laney looks at me with relief and says blood will tell!

Anyway, I couldn't make Annie believe I wouldn't go off the rails any time the adrenalin started pumping, so I gave up trying.

She'd promised to write, and she had, at first. But then the series was over, two months ahead of schedule, and she wanted to stay and see what all this fuss about a white Christmas was and the BBC had offered her a job—she knew I'd understand. And then, nothing. Oh, one brief postcard in February. She was working on *White's Wilderness* with ecologist Damien White, they were off to Spain, she was up to her ears, she didn't know when she'd be home —over and out!

Peta Ryde was Annie's best friend and had moved into her flat while she was away to look after her pot plants. I liked Peta, but lately I couldn't pass her door without remembering and thinking she was probably hearing news more regularly which my pride wouldn't let me ask about. I began to avoid her, feeling nervy when we accidentally met, jumping out of my skin when she caught me up on the stairs saying, 'Micky! Wait a minute, have I got news for you!' When my heart had slowed down I'd realized it wasn't about Annie. Monica was redecorating and we could say what colours we'd like for the hall and corridors.

I began to feel frustated, abandoned, lost and sorry for myself. Surely Annie would write, surely she'd be missing me and coming home soon. That was the one exception to my otherwise pretty comfortable life, which caused a vague, familiar ache somewhere inside me, even on the best days, and threw a small, permanent rain cloud on to my horizon.

Each mail brought no relief until today—and she'd told Peta first, not me! Even the most irritating optimist couldn't say that augured well for my future.

However, I wasn't the only one with problems. That night, on the Southside, someone chucked a bomb into the front garden of leading conservationist Hugh Grant. Lucky for him he'd heard a noise and gone out the back to investigate.

CHAPTER 2

The pale blue aerogram arrived next morning. I turned it over, heart thumping. On the back, Annie had scrawled, 'Micky, I'm so sorry! Meant to post this a week ago. Just found it in my bag. Better late than never. Love, Annie.' I grinned with relief. The date inside the letter confirmed that it would have arrived five days earlier. I breathed a silent apology to Annie and read her message.

She was sorry she hadn't written for so long. After Spain, she'd found herself in the middle of the African bush with Damien White, filming a story about the Kalahari bush-men. They'd been quite isolated, living off the land with their small, gentle hosts. It was part of a series about unique places on the planet. And now—was I sitting down?—they were coming to Australia to film Mitchell Island! She'd be writing to Peta to see if she could stay in her old flat for a couple of days. They were bringing a crew, including a Dutchman, Hank Jansen, who was a brilliant wildlife photographer and a dear friend. They'd been together with Damien in Africa. A knife twisted in my gut. One thing was quite clear. Hank Jansen and I were not going to be friends. Somehow I read a threat in the excited rush of words; Annie, unchanged in that respect at least, bubbling over with excitement, giving herself away . . . I shook myself angrily. I was behaving like a schoolboy, jealously on the defensive. She was bound to have other male friends and she didn't belong to me. There'd been no promises between us.

I forced myself back to the letter, checking the day and time of arrival. I'd be there, I promised myself grimly. I'd be at the airport waiting for my Annie, and Hank Bloody Jansen had better watch himself.

Monica was delighted with my news. 'I *thought* Peta said

Damien White! He's marvellous! I never miss *White's Wilderness* on TV. I suppose they're doing Mitchell Island because of the proposed World Heritage listing. It's a unique place, and beautiful. I spent a week at a resort there a few years ago—before all the trouble between the Greenies and the loggers.'

She was also bubbling over with excitement and dragged me into her flat.

'If you attack me, I'll scream,' I warned her.

She blew me a kiss. 'Silly boy! Just look and see what I've got!'

'Etchings?'

'Behave, Micky! Look!'

The painting had pride of place on her wall. I studied it with growing enjoyment. It was a forest scene. The late afternoon sunlight shafted through the trees, creating a golden-green effect so you could breathe the warmth and the sweetness of it. A sandy path, mottled and flecked with sun and shadow, invited the viewer to follow into the quiet depths of the painting. The artist had caught the light to perfection and it glowed from every tree-trunk.

I grinned at Monica. 'Well, I was nearly right. It's brilliant, love!'

'Mmmm! Isn't it, though! Oh, Micky, it's a Margaret Yates.'

I studied the signature. 'Good God! So it is, you lucky devil.'

'I saw it in Fields' Gallery. I've always wanted a Yates so I plucked up enough courage to ask the price.' She grimaced. 'It wasn't cheap, but I did love it so much—so I took the plunge and splurged.'

'It's an investment. With her reputation and all the mystery, it'll only increase in value. Well done, Monica.'

Margaret Yates is a local artist, as eccentric as they come and as famous as Sawrey or Drysdale. Always contemptuous of the glitz that went with success, she never gave interviews, and never attended her shows, giving that task to

Martin Fields, gallery owner and agent. One day, tired of people and the press, she murmured, 'I vant to be alone,' and disappeared, seemingly off the face of the map. Only Fields knew where she'd hidden herself and he withstood all efforts to make him talk, including, so rumour had it, some very substantial bribes. So Margaret Yates, veiled in mystery, retired from the world and once in a while Fields receives a new batch of paintings which are snapped up by eager collectors without so much as a wince at the huge prices asked.

I left Monica, feeling more cheerful than I'd been for months. Annie was coming home, she'd not dropped me after all and perhaps this time I'd persuade her to stay. I'd not stray from the straight and narrow, I promised myself. If the god of trouble walked right up the stairs and into my flat, I'd not get involved. I was well due for a little peace of mind to sort out my private life, anyway.

I had to wait until that evening to see Peta. She works in an office in the city. I'd not seen much of her in the months she'd been at No. 18. She had a busy social life outside working hours and I'd noticed her going out in the evenings with at least three different men, so I figured there was nobody special in her life. She was involved in local amateur theatricals with the Paddington Players and a couple of times we tenants had gone along in a group to see her performing.

She'd made various friendly overtures when she'd first arrived, even inviting me down to No. 4 for dinner. I'd accepted, but being in Annie's flat put a damper on my evening although Peta went out of her way to make the dinner a success with candles and champagne. She was pretty and bright and fun to be with, but I felt disloyal to Annie whenever I was with Peta and I backed off, declining her invitations, putting her firmly in the position of acquaintance rather than friend. She and Monica had become very close and Monica seemed to make a point of bringing Peta up in our conversations, keeping me informed of her doings.

'She likes you, Micky,' she told me one day, about three months after Peta had moved in.

'Well, I like her too. She's a good neighbour and always remembers to leave the laundry tidy.'

Monica gave me a look but didn't pursue the subject.

Peta opened her door, glossy black hair swinging to her shoulders, glasses perched on the tip of her nose. She's one of those vibrant, glowing people, dark eyes sparkling behind enormous rainbow-rimmed glasses, olive skin tanned to warm brown, her mouth red without any artificial colouring. She smiled gladly at me, surprised but pleased.

'Micky! Come in, stranger. You know, I thought you'd been avoiding me.'

'Now, would I!' I smiled suavely and hoped she'd not notice my red face as I entered the familiar flat. Peta hadn't changed things much; only put her own knick-knacks about, but for the rest, it was still Annie's place. This time I was happy to be there, even with all the memories crowding in with me.

'I gather you know Annie's coming back,' I said, not very truthfully, but I wasn't prepared to come clean. 'She said she'd be writing to you.'

Peta nodded. 'Yes, I got her letter. Coffee, Micky?'

'Thanks. I'll be going to the airport to meet her, of course. Do you want to come with me?'

She paused in her coffee-making and looked at me thoughtfully over her rainbow glasses. 'I was planning to go, but I'll take the Moke. Apparently there'll be six of them, and heaps of baggage, equipment, all that sort of thing. We'll need two vehicles. But thanks for thinking of me.'

I accepted the mug she held out. 'You realize all the media will be at the airport as well,' she continued. 'Damien White's bound to give a press conference. He's ultra big news, especially now, with such a worldwide interest in saving the planet.'

'Ah!' I hadn't thought of that. 'They wouldn't have arranged transport already, I suppose?'

'Didn't Annie tell you?' She looked surprised. 'I don't know. If they have, we'll simply kidnap Annie and bring her home with us.'

I finished my coffee thinking, careful, you nearly blew it! Loose lips sink ships and you nearly scuppered yours! Peta took the empty mug, watching me with an expression that was hard to fathom. Then she said abruptly, 'It's always been Annie, hasn't it?'

I looked at her, thinking, what the . . . ! 'Yes,' I said gently, 'since I first met her, it's always been Annie.'

'Well, I wish you two would get together and make it permanent,' she said, and laughed lightly. 'For the sake of all the frustrated girls, if nothing else.'

I laughed with her, said a couple of non-committal things, and headed back to No. 5. Well, I'll be damned! I thought. Peta could be a very disturbing lady. I was annoyed at myself for the sudden unbidden thought that had flickered in my mind in response to the look in her eyes; and with Annie coming home and all!

CHAPTER 3

Carnie and I watched the evening news. She likes the tennis. Fancies herself a Navratilova or Graf. Hugh Grant, shaken but not stirred, was interviewed and, in his gentle way, gave it as his opinion that it was a pity those interest groups opposed to the Mitchell Island World Heritage listing should have allowed their emotions to get the better of them, when he was always available to discuss the issues and this would only prejudice the inquiry. I watched him, wondering as always how this mild-mannered man with the thin, rounded shoulders, wispy greying hair and heavy black-framed glasses ever had the nerve to stand in front of bulldozers, tie himself to trees, write slogans on the walls of Parliament House and take the Government to court, conduct his own case, and win!

He peered at the reporter, eyes enlarged behind thick lenses, giving him the air of a short-sighted, anxious mouse.

'Do you know for certain that the bomb was the work of these alleged interest groups?'

Grant put two fingers to his mouth as if afraid something would pop out of its own accord. 'Well, I had a letter two days previously,' he said carefully, 'to the effect that I'd better not try to stop the logging on Mitchell Island. The police have it now, and will no doubt discover who sent it.'

'Has this threat and its violent aftermath caused you to re-think your position on Mitchell Island?'

'Absolutely not!' The soft voice grew more emphatic. 'It's vital that the logging of the rainforest be stopped, and stopped now. I believe the island can regenerate—it's not too late, but every day logging continues is adding another hundred years to what it needs to recover.'

Grant was sitting straight in his chair now, eyes suddenly snapping, his conviction giving him an extraordinary strength and energy. The reporter blinked and drew back slightly.

'So the battle is still on?'

Grant looked full into the camera, a half smile on his lips. 'It's never been off,' he said quietly. 'And, as you know, I've never been one to run from trouble.'

I grinned at the TV. 'Them's fighting words, Grant,' I told his close-up. 'Rather you than me!'

The phone rang just then, so I left Carnie to get the end of the story. A familiar, breezy voice charged through the wires.

'G'day, my old son!'

'Duke!'

'The very same,' he agreed, 'although I'm amazed you still remember me.'

'Eh?' I was baffled.

'You're a mean bastard,' he complained, 'holding out on your best mate!'

'Duke, what *are* you on about?'

'Only that you've got Damien White arriving and not a word to a soul.'

'You madman! I only heard myself today. How the hell did you . . . ?'

'Annie,' he told me. 'Sent me a press release, the dear girl. She still knows who her friends are.'

'Well, you'll know more than me—or at least as much. Apparently he's coming with a crew to do a documentary on Mitchell Island.'

'Then I hope he doesn't go stirring the possum over there,' Duke said thoughtfully. 'It's getting more than a bit of a bun fight and the Greenies would love to get a heavy-weight like White on side. God knows what they'd do then —under the heading of the end justifying the means.'

'Not Greenie mad, I take it?' I asked him curiously. There'd been a sardonic note in his voice.

'Not fanatic mad,' he corrected. 'I suppose you heard about Hugh Grant's bomb.'

'On the news just now. The loggers, apparently.'

'Maybe.' Duke was non-committal. 'It's never that simple, or neatly cut and dried. Interest groups are everywhere and perhaps some of them would be willing to set others up to take the rap.'

'You've got inside info,' I guessed. 'Is it one of your cases?'

'Indirectly. Hugh's a mate of mine. He asked me to do some quiet investigating on my own; unofficial, of course.'

'Well, that'll be right up your street. I wish you success.'

'So! Your Annie's coming back.' Duke switched the subject abruptly. 'Give me all the news!'

When I got back to the TV, Carnie was watching her favourite game, head jerking from side to side, paw out to catch the ball in case it escaped from Centre Court into our living-room. A real pro!

I thought about Duke, smiling to myself. We grew up together; went to the same school, tried to marry the same girl, Francesca Bellini, daughter of Luigi who runs our favourite pizzeria. Duke won. He mostly did, but it never led to any dissension between us. He's the most alive person I ever knew; energy seems to crackle through him, driving his restless spirit around the globe in his pursuit of a good story. Duke's a journalist. You'd know him as Richard Jordan. He came by his nickname at school from swaggering around with his thumbs hooked into an imaginary gun belt, drawling 'You'd better believe it, mister,' in imitation of his hero. Duke's been in trouble all over the world. In Nicaragua, observing from the front line of the Government forces, he was captured by the Contras, not only charming his way out from in front of a firing squad, but getting an armed escort to see him safely over the border and out of strife. He was in Tiananmen Square on that 4th of June, lying on the back seat of a parked car while the People's Army massacred the people's children. That exploit won him yet another Walkley Award for journalism and he escaped with nothing more serious than a bullet in the shoulder and a cudgel to the head. I told him he was the luckiest man I knew.

'More lives than a cat!'

He looked at me seriously for a moment, then his deep grey eyes crinkled at the corners and he ran his hand through this thick brown mop of hair, embarrassed.

'Y'know, Micky, sometimes, when I hit a spot of bother, like that bloody Chinese affair, it seems like there's something—or someone—with me, sort of protecting me. I, well, I just *know* I'm going to be OK—and you probably think I'm mad as a bloody meat axe, and if you so much as smirk, I'll punch your lights out, pilgrim!'

Just the same, I'd had my anxious moments about Duke, whatever god of protection he thought he had on his side. Just now, for instance. It was all right for Grant, a single man living on his own. He could play ducks and drakes with his life. But Duke had Francesca and their daughter Maria and he was still taking stupid risks and getting involved with God knows what causes, because he couldn't stand to see 'little blokes getting picked on', and he had a passion for justice that pulled him headlong into the excitement and danger he seemed to crave. Well, I couldn't condemn him for that. To tell the truth, I'm a bit that way myself! I knew he'd resent any suggestion that he couldn't look after Fran and my god-daughter but, just the same, it bothered me that he was now apparently rushing headlong into the Mitchell Island affair; and, if the Greenies had any idea of involving Damien White in their politics, Annie, by her association with the ecologist, would also be involved and that would make two people I cared a lot about, which was two too many. I sighed. I'd just have to keep an eye on both of them. I was not a happy person!

CHAPTER 4

Saturday, 9.30 in the morning and the International Terminal was buzzing. Outside in the still, cool morning a vocal group with green headbands and placards proclaimed HANDS OFF MITCHELL ISLAND, and DON'T DESTROY THE NATION'S HERITAGE. A little way down the road from the visitors' car park several harassed policemen were trying to convince a second vocal group with hard hats that they couldn't bring their bulldozer in here and block traffic which had a legitimate right to access the airport. Their placards read LOGGING EQUALS JOBS and SUSTAINABLE YIELD PROTECTS FORESTS. I looked around nervously but there were no bombs in evidence. Peta and I dodged a police van arriving with reinforcements and made it to the door, which slid open politely before we got there and closed with a certain automatic flair behind our backs.

'Shit! said Peta, with feeling.

Inside, a little band of reporters and TV cameramen waited by the Customs gate, among them a tall, dark-haired bloke who was striding restlessly about, swapping a word here, a comment there. He waved and spoke briefly to a thin, round-shouldered, bespectacled man before crossing to meet us.

'Duke Jordan, Peta Ryde,' I supplied, and she looked at him wide-eyed as she put out her hand.

'*Richard* Jordan? *The* Richard Jordan?'

'The very same,' I said, adding with what I felt was justifiable annoyance, 'That's Hugh Grant! How did he get in? The crazies are being kept outside.'

Duke winked at Peta. 'Not worried about the odd explosion, are you, mate?' he asked me with a comical look. 'Hugh's not one of the crazies. He's a respected conservationist, not a radical. He's here to meet Damien White —at White's request, I might add.'

'He invites trouble,' I said shortly. 'It's building up outside.'

'The police can handle it. So! Won't be long to wait. They're being whipped through Customs.'

A stir at the gate made me forget Grant and his Greenies. I moved quickly forward to join the waiting crowd, eyes searching for the only face I wanted to see. A few people came through and were claimed by excited relatives and friends. The tannoy sprang to life to deliver a completely indistinguishable message; then she was there and every-thing else was forgotten. Her white-gold hair was cut boyishly short, her skin was the colour of ripe honey. A tall man behind her put his hand on her shoulder in an offici-ously protective way and she glanced up at him and smiled with a warmth that set my teeth on edge. I looked him over with irritation. He had the look of an outdoor type, well muscled and tanned. Shoulder-length fair hair was tied back at the nape of his neck and he sported a short, curly blond beard and moustache. He moved with the uncon-scious grace of a wild animal and I sensed that, like a wild animal, he could be a dangerous man in a tight corner. I suppose he was handsome in a rugged, Viking way, if you like that sort of thing.

In the centre of the group with Annie was a shorter man with a familiar face. Damien White was smaller than I'd expected, not more than five foot eight, and far more groomed than he appeared on TV, where I'd seen him looking as if he'd been dragged through several bushes, playing with chimpanzees in the wild, picking up deadly snakes with aplomb and discussing poisonous spiders within an inch of their lairs. He also looked older. And they say the camera doesn't lie!

Annie saw me through the press of reporters and curious onlookers and waved. Several airport officials appeared and took charge, whisking the film crew and its star off to the

VIP lounge, followed by the media. After a hurried discussion, Annie broke free and came towards me. I caught
my breath. I'd forgotten how beautiful she was—and the
way she walked so lightly, even in jeans, and probably with
jet lag.

I felt Peta watching us but I only had eyes for one person.
She stopped in front of me and I took her hands, feeling
clumsy and stupid and afraid of what my voice would do if
I spoke.

'Micky! How wonderful to see you again!' She laughed
up at me, her green eyes glowing. The little hazel flecks
were still there, I noticed; then she was hugging me and
Peta and she reached up and kissed my cheek and said,
'You look struck all of a heap!'

I held her a little longer than I'd meant to and she gave
me a swift look from under her lashes. I'd not been prepared
for the sudden snap of my nerves and the sharp ache inside
me. She linked arms with us both as I fought to pull myself
together and clear my throat.

'I excused myself from the press conference. After all,
they didn't want me, only Damien. It's so good to be home.
Let's grab a coffee while we wait for the boss.'

We found a table in the coffee shop where we could see
the door of the VIP lounge. As we chatted and Peta and I
brought Annie up to date with the home news, I watched
her covertly. The short, spiky hair made her look elfin and
suited her, but I thought the changes went deeper than just
surface. She seemed more casual in her dress and manner.
My neat, trim Annie now stretched out legs encased in
worn blue denim and pushed back the sleeves of a sloppy
joe. A scarf was knotted loosely around her neck and she
carried a canvas shoulder-bag. Her eyes met mine and she
put a hand to her head, laughing.

'I know, you hate it! You'd prefer long, silky tresses. But
it's practical. You can't get a shampoo and set in the jungle.
Appearance doesn't matter.'

'No, I actually like it—on you,' I said quickly. 'I'm not as old-fashioned as that.'

She grimaced at Peta. 'Don't you believe it,' she told her. 'He hasn't caught up with Women's Lib yet.'

'I know.' Peta looked slightly troubled. 'I like it. There aren't too many gentlemen left, these days.'

'I'm an endangered species,' I joked, aware of a sudden tension. 'Your boss should try to save me, too.'

The door of the VIP lounge opened and various media members hurried out, all wanting to be first back to base with the news. The big man I'd seen with Annie was among them and, as the space around him cleared, stood irresolute, looking about.

Annie waved and beckoned and he grinned and headed our way with his long stride. I frowned, catching at a wayward thought. Sensual, that was it. I wondered vaguely how I walked and dismissed the idea angrily. The last thing I wanted to do was to compare myself with this man.

He joined us, seeming to crowd our small table with his presence. He smiled crookedly at me as Annie introduced us.

'Jansen,' I acknowledged. She'd pronounced it Yonsen.

'So this is the Micky Douglas we hear so much about.' He extended his hand and I felt his latent strength. God grant me patience, I was going to be pleasant to the bastard! After all, he was a guest in my country and with luck he wouldn't be here that long. I wondered, if he'd heard about me, why hadn't I heard about him? I hoped I could take comfort from the thought that Annie talked about me.

'Conference over?' I asked.

'For the media, yes.' He signalled a waitress and ordered coffee. 'Now the boss is talking with Hugh Grant. He asks me to arrange somewhere for them to continue, away from here, and not at the hotel just yet. We've been told there are demonstrators there as well.' He stretched and yawned widely. 'How I hate to be cooped up on these long flights. It will be good to leave and stretch our legs.'

'Why don't we go back to my flat?' I suggested. The more I kept him under my eye, the better.

'That would be ideal,' Annie agreed. 'Could you stand us all?'

I smiled warmly at her. 'A pleasure, love.'

Jansen watched this exchange and grinned. 'It would be most welcome. Thank you.'

'I'll tell Damien.' Annie rose quickly and made her way across the terminal. Jansen and I watched her, thoughtfully.

'A beautiful girl, Annie,' he said quietly.

'She certainly is.' I looked at him but he just smiled blandly with no hint that he'd understood and accepted the challenge.

CHAPTER 5

Outside the air was hotting up as the sun baked the expanses of concrete and tarmac, although tropical trees made welcome shade patches. Peta and I somehow squeezed the group plus a mountain of baggage into our two vehicles, which we'd driven to the Terminal doors to avoid the demonstrators.

'Oh, great, you've still got the Capri!' Annie said, pleased. 'I'll come with you, Micky.'

'Me, too.' Jansen followed her, with a backwards glance at me.

Duke nodded at Grant. 'You'd better come with me, Hugh. We don't want to stir anybody up by having you seen with Mr White.'

Damien White smiled. 'It seems to me that if people want to be stirred up, they'll find their own reasons,' he said, 'but in view of the current ill-feeling, it seems wise. I'll join you, Mr Douglas, if I may.'

Jansen sat beside me, filling the passenger seat, while Annie and Damien White were crushed together in the back. 1971 Ford Capris aren't noted for their palatial back quarters. Anyway, I told myself grimly, it was safer than crushing Annie and Jansen together. The demonstrators recognized the TV personality and began to shout to him, slogans for and against logging getting jumbled together. Some girls in the Green group began to scream and push against the police who moved in, arms linked. A scuffle broke out and White tapped my shoulder.

'Let me out. I'll talk to them. We can't have this.'

'Is that wise?' I began, but it wasn't my business, so I got out and folded down the seat for him. Duke, walking off with Grant, did an about turn and followed White across to the seething demonstrators. Some of the loggers, realizing what was happening, broke free of the police and began to sprint over.

I got back into the Capri, feeling slightly stunned.

'He'll be fine,' Annie assured me. 'He's got a gift with people. He meets this sort of thing all the time. He can do it with wild animals, too. I've seen him walk up to an angry and dangerous animal and just talk to it and soothe it until it's almost tame.'

She seemed to be right. No one was throwing any bombs, anyway, and the noise had quietened down. We could hear White's voice carrying clearly to the crowd.

'I'm not here to take sides on this issue,' he told them. 'I'm here to film a unique piece of wilderness. The island belongs to you, and you, the people of Queensland, must decide its fate together. I hope you will be able to put aside your personal interests and discuss rationally what is best for all concerned. I believe there is shortly to be a Government inquiry.' Here voices began shouting, some in derision. White held up his hand and, miraculously, the voices were silenced.

'No good will be gained from dissension,' he said. 'World affairs clearly demonstrate that violence breeds violence. Overcome your personal fears and talk together. There may be many possible solutions which will need good will to bring about. You know me,' he continued. 'I will listen to all sides and my documentary will be fair and unbiased. I will not, however, be used in your battles or claimed by any side.'

Someone shouted, 'I thought you were on the side of wilderness!'

'The wilderness cannot be saved through violence and anger,' he replied gravely, 'but only by humanity, working together for the good of all. That is my only interest. Now I ask you to disperse. I will be meeting with all your group leaders in the course of my stay here. I would like to see you leave peacefully. Will you do that?'

His voice was warm, hypnotic. One by one they moved

away and White just stood and watched them, smiling, shaking their hands, thanking them. The police, bemused, began to break up the demonstrators and see them off. White strolled back to the car.

'That's it,' he said cheerfully. 'Shall we go? I'd love a cup of tea.'

Duke beat us back to No. 18 and when we arrived, he and Hugh Grant were chatting with Monica in the foyer. Monica hugged Annie and held out her hand delightedly as we introduced her to her hero.

'Mr White! I'm thrilled to meet you!' she told him. 'I'm a great fan of yours. I love your show—it's my favourite.'

He smiled at her. 'It's extremely kind of you to say so, Mrs Wainwright. Would you care to join us for a cup of tea? Mr Douglas has offered to refresh us all.' He looked at me. 'Is that in order, Mr Douglas?'

'Of course.' I grinned at Monica. 'Come on up, love.'

Carnie took one look at the invasion and retired in high dudgeon to her basket as Peta helped me settle my guests and brew coffee and tea. Besides Annie, Jansen and Damien White there was Craig Edgeley, the sound engineer, a tall, thin, stick insect of a man, Melody Scott, a short, plump girl with sandy hair and brows and soft brown eyes, who was the scriptwriter, and a black-haired Irishman, Paddy O'Hara.

'Short for Padraic, like the sainted Pearse himself,' he told me in his soft brogue. 'I'm after being the general help around this outfit and can turn me hands to just about anything you'd wish to try me at. Thank you kindly, Micky, I'll admit to having a thirst to me and I could stand to take a drink; but I wouldn't say no to a drop of that sweet-smelling coffee you've got fresh on the brew, so if you'll just slip the one inside of t'other, I'll be as happy as a man could be.'

I took him at his word and laced his coffee with Scotch, and he grinned appreciatively.

'It's a fine man you are,' he approved. 'Here's to yer health!'

'That was quite a display, at the airport,' Duke said drily.

'They are all afraid,' White explained. 'It's the old story. The loggers fear their livelihood will be taken from them and they have families to support, the conservationists fear the destruction of the forest, and the planet itself, and both sides are sure they are right. So naturally, where fear is involved, tempers become frayed.'

'It hasn't been like that,' Grant interrupted. 'The one thing that has been outstanding with the Mitchell Island situation is that it's been generally peaceful and good-natured. All sides have been having dialogue. Sure, the Greenies have moved on to the island and have been demonstrating and blocking the logging roads, but the loggers so far have taken it in good part and have been simply moving to another area without confrontation. It's not like the violent protests in the New South Wales forests. I'd say it's been a perfect example of peaceful demonstration.'

'That's true,' Duke agreed. 'Lionel Blake, QC, the man heading the Government Inquiry into the future of logging on the island, has a reputation for fairness and common sense, so people are generally prepared to wait and see what his recommendations will be before they start anything.'

'Then who threw the bomb?' White asked quietly.

'Ah, there you have it,' Grant smiled. 'The loggers have denied it, of course. The warning letter was posted in Eversleigh—but that's not to go beyond this room, please.'

Annie gasped. 'But that's where —'

'Exactly, Miss Mason. Eversleigh is the loggers' base— a timber town.'

I frowned. 'Isn't that a bit obvious?' I asked slowly.

Grant beamed at me. 'Exactly,' he repeated. 'Far too obvious. If the loggers or any of the timber interests wanted to make a threat and remain anonymous, they'd hardly post the letter from their very own town.'

'On the other hand,' I put in, 'if they wanted to announce themselves, to let you know exactly what you were up against, they might very well do so.'

Damien White looked at us with interest. 'Presumably any group wishing to discredit the loggers could do the same.'

'You've got it, White,' Duke approved. 'In fact, it could be anyone at all.'

'Except the police tell me it was not an amateurish affair,' Grant said. 'A highly sophisticated device, apparently. If I'd been in bed, where I had been not five minutes before the explosion, I'd be definitely on the side of the angels by now.'

White leaned forward. 'And what would the Government Inquiry reaction have been to that?'

Grant and Duke looked at each other. 'That's an interesting thought,' Duke said. 'Could it have been more to influence the Inquiry than to get at you, Hugh?'

'Five minutes earlier and it would have been the same thing,' Grant said caustically. 'However, I'm still very much alive, so I suppose, if I'm the target, they'll try again.'

'Sure now, that's not a comforting thought to take to yer bed with,' Paddy said, grinning. 'Would somebody be telling us more about this Eversleigh place and Mitchell Island? If I'm in the path of a bomb or three, I like to know who's throwing them and why.'

CHAPTER 6

Grant put two fingers to his lips and gathered his thoughts. 'It's an interesting history,' he said, 'geologically and politically. For one thing, it's a sand island. It was once joined to the mainland—indeed, probably has been many times since its formation, some four hundred thousand years ago. Changing sea levels, you understand, cause it to be isolated at times. The last time the sea rose was, oh, seven thousand years ago, give or take.'

'I used to go there for holidays,' Annie put in. 'There's only one genuine rocky area and that has salt-water pools. We used to explore them when I was a kid.'

'That's right.' Grant nodded. 'All the rest is sand; even the two areas known as Mariner's Rock and Fisherman's Head Rock are really highly compressed sand.'

'There are Aboriginal sites,' Monica said. 'Middens. I saw them when I was there.'

'Yes, it's believed there were Aboriginals on the island at least fifty thousand years ago.' Grant turned to Damien White. Beside him, Melody Scott was scribbling away in a stenographer's pad, taking notes of the conversation. 'The middens are mostly piles of pippy shells. The Aboriginals continually inhabited the island until the white men came.'

'They were driven off,' Annie said, 'by the timber cutters. They wanted the island for themselves.'

'It was during the gold rushes to North Queensland,' Grant explained. 'The mainland was being populated and, of course, the settlers saw all that magnificent timber, just across the water and easily accessible by boat. It must have been quite spectacular. Huge trees, two to three thousand years old—satinays, white beech, blackbutt, tallow wood, brush box, and the pines. Hoop, kauri . . .' He looked at us dreamily. 'It must have seemed like the Garden of Eden.

There are over one hundred species of trees on the island
today. Who knows how many more then. It would have
been impossible to believe the supply could ever run out.
Just standing there from Creation and free for the taking.
Arthur Eversleigh saw a golden opportunity and started
cutting the timber and floating the logs across to the mainland. That was in 1870. He founded the town of Eversleigh
and his descendants still run the timber mill there. Old
Tom Eversleigh owns it now and his son Brent manages
the mill. They're decent people. In their own way they care
for the island: they've been there for a hundred and twenty
years so they feel they've as much claim as anyone. But
their family logged the timber unmercifully and all the old
trees are gone now. You'll see a few as old as five hundred
years, maybe a bit more, but they destroyed the giants. All
for a few lousy bucks.' He shook his head sadly.

Duke, never able to sit still for long, stood up abruptly and
walked to the window which overlooked the front of the house,
the small park across the road and the giant fig tree which
spends a sedentary life quietly ripping up the footpath.

'The trouble is,' he said over his shoulder, 'that four
hundred-odd people in Eversleigh depend on the timber
industry for their livelihood. The mill workers, contract
loggers, their families, the local business people—they've
prospered because of the Island for over a century and they
feel they have a right to continue to live and work in their
town.' He grinned at White, his mobile face twisting comi-
cally. 'You'll find Queensland country towns very par-
ochial,' he warned him. 'If your family hasn't been there
for at least a hundred years, you're an outsider. They can
give you a hard time, just by letting you know you're not
one of them. They're strictly conservative and you aren't
likely to be flavour of the month. Whether you like it or
not, they'll brand you a Greenie and see you as a threat.'

'What about the Eversleighs themselves?' White looked
at Hugh Grant, eyebrows raised. 'You said they care for
the island.'

'With the emphasis on "in their own way".' Grant nodded. 'As I said, Arthur Eversleigh started the timber industry. He set up a little mill on Mitchell Island in 1885, but he couldn't get men to stay in the isolation, especially with hostile blacks lurking in the forests. So he shifted his operations to the mainland and went back to lashing the logs together and rafting them over. Towed them behind the barges. The settlement was known as "Eversleigh's Mill", now just Eversleigh. Tom Eversleigh is obviously interested in logging continuing and has put together quite a case for the Inquiry. He claims that the loggers are responsible people and that the forests certainly aren't going to disappear. The Eversleighs employ a hundred people, which is vital for the town, and they practise the sustainable yield system.'

Monica cast a look of entreaty at Damien White, who smiled at her. 'It's the practice of taking from a forest only what that forest will reproduce,' he said. 'It's an excellent method and a sensible way to approach conservation, to allow your resource to continually renew itself. It began in Germany, which had destroyed its forests to the extent that the Germans had to import timber. It worked so well for them that now they export timber to the rest of Europe.'

Grant coughed and touched his lip. 'The Eversleighs aren't hostile to the conservation groups,' he said. 'They feel kinship with them, rather. They certainly believe logging isn't harming the forest—they see themselves as its protectors, if anything. They say if it wasn't for them, the tourists would cause no end of damage.'

Hank Jensen looked up. 'And there are many tourists?' he asked. At the sound of his deep voice Carnie suddenly stepped daintily out of her basket and went to him, rubbing around his legs before leaping gracefully into his lap and rearranging it for her comfort. He gave his crooked grin and began to stroke her. 'Nice cat, Douglas,' he said.

Traitor, I told Carnie silently. If you cats are so bloody psychic, what are you doing in the enemy's lap?

Grant was explaining that tourists were a major problem.

'They come each year in their thousands and the back-packers go everywhere. And since the blockades started, there are even more of them, sensation-seekers, all avid to see trouble. I reckon jobs could be easily replaced by employing people to police the island and encouraging tourism to Eversleigh; get it back on to the mainland. Mitchell should be preserved for what it is—a beautiful piece of wilderness.'

Duke turned from the window and sat down again. 'You've got Hugh started on his hobby-horse now,' he complained with a twinkle. 'Don't you know he took the Government to court over this issue?'

White nodded. 'I know quite a lot about Mr Grant's work for the forests,' he said. 'It was about a land sale, I believe.'

Grant nodded. 'All very hush-hush,' he explained. 'The Government of the day was about to sell a huge area of the Island to a joint Japanese/Australian venture to run a really big tourist resort over there. Five-star hotel, 18-hole golf course, acres of forest to be clear felled. It was a scandal.' He smiled modestly. 'Luckily the scheme was leaked to me by a horrified civil servant in the Department of Tourism and I put a stop to it.'

'That must have made you the popular boy,' O'Hara remarked.

'They went the whole hog—death threats and the works,' Grant agreed, 'but, until now, no one's ever thrown a bomb at me. The company cut its losses and took itself off.'

Craig Edgeley stirred. He'd been listening quietly to all this, long, thin legs stretched out in front of him, chin resting on bony clasped hands.

'Isn't there already tourism on the island?' he asked, in a clipped Oxbridge voice. 'I believe we're booked into a Paradise Palms motel.'

'Oh yes, there's a small group of residents and three tourist operations, but they're limited to about thirty guests at any time and are on the foreshores. The residents aren't a problem. They'd like most of the tourists to be based off the island, because they went there originally for peace and quiet. There are some eccentrics, a couple of home industries making souvenirs and one or two millionaires who enjoy the fishing.'

I winced. I've never been one for blood sports. Fishes the world over have nothing to fear from me.

Damien White turned to Grant and smiled slightly. 'Well, Mr Grant, it seems you were quite right,' he told him. 'There'll be plenty of material for me here. I've a feeling I'm going to enjoy this trip.'

Duke grinned at me. 'Yes, old son, Hugh invited this lot to take a look at Mitchell Island. All good publicity for his cause.'

I glared at him. 'Then you knew all along,' I said accusingly. 'You were just winding me up on the phone.'

'Couldn't resist it.' He winked. 'But Annie did send me a press release. Mr White was delighted to accept Hugh's offer.'

'On condition that I speak to all parties involved and film their stories,' White agreed. 'Mr Grant obliged and has set up interviews for me with—Melody?'

Melody Scott flipped back through her pad and said briefly, 'Mr Hugh Grant, representing the conservationists; Mr Sinclair Faraday, the Forestry Department; Mr Les Brown, logging contractor; Miss Susan Murray of Paradise Palms resort; Mr Brent Eversleigh, manager of Eversleigh and Sons Proprietary Limited.'

The phone rang and I got up to answer it.

'It's Fran, Duke.'

Duke took the receiver. 'I stopped at a phone-box to let her know I'd be here.'

'We transfer to the island in two days,' Melody continued. 'That will give us ample time to make our initial research and begin our interviews. We have an appointment with Mr Brent Eversleigh this afternoon. He has kindly agreed to come to Brisbane to meet us.'

'Sorry, folks!' Duke hung up looking decidedly grim. 'The meeting's off. Brent Eversleigh was run down by a car this morning. He's in the Eversleigh hospital with multiple fractures. They reckon it's touch and go if he'll pull through.'

CHAPTER 7

After Duke had taken himself off at top speed to learn more about the accident, the gathering broke up. Peta and I drove White and his crew into town, startled to see the build-up of demonstrators on the footpath opposite the hotel. They'd already tried to present a petition to the celebrity, retreating only after being informed by the manager that White hadn't arrived yet. They'd promised to try again later. Annie stayed with her friends to see them settled in and we arranged to meet for dinner at Luigi's where, with any luck, we'd get a meal in peace—if they could dodge the watchers outside the Sheraton. Meanwhile, Grant would try to organize another interview for the ecologist.

Duke phoned after lunch. 'He's still alive,' he said abruptly. 'There were plenty of eyewitnesses. Happened smack in the middle of the main street, outside the Eversleigh Railway Station. It was a hit and run, probably a deliberate attempt to kill him. He was crossing the street to catch the train to Brisbane and the vehicle went for him full bore. A four-wheel drive job. One of the witnesses got the number and the police have picked up the culprits.'

'Already?' I was impressed.

'It wasn't difficult. They walked into the police station themselves, claiming their vehicle had been stolen. The police had got a pretty good description and the pair fitted it to a T. Both were wearing green headbands, the uniform of MICO, the Mitchell Island Conservation Organization. They must have hidden the vehicle somewhere and thought they could bluff the cops into thinking it had been nicked.'

'That was pretty stupid.'

'If criminals didn't do pretty stupid things, most crimes would never be solved. Psychiatrists say it's deliberate—

unconscious, of course. They feel guilty and want to be caught and punished.'

All the same, I was curious. If I'd just run down one of Eversleigh's leading citizens the last thing I'd have tried would be the sort of bluff a child could see through.

'What did they say when they were told they'd been recognized?' I asked Duke.

'Denied it, of course. Stuck to their story. They'd come up to join the green blockade of the island, had an hour to kill before the ferry arrived, so left their Land-Rover on the jetty to be first in line and went for a walk. When they returned they found the Rover gone and went to the police. But their description was given to the police by several people. It tallies, as far as eyewitness accounts ever tally.'

'What was the description? Was it really enough to identify them?' I was wondering how much I'd have noticed in that situation.

'It's certainly enough to hold them for questioning,' Duke said. 'A couple, male and female, green headbands, male, brown hair and beard, female, long brown hair, both wearing what was described as "hippy" gear.'

'Sounds like the vast majority of Greenies I've ever seen,' I remarked.

'True. However, it was their vehicle and I wonder if anyone in MICO would deliberately steal another member's car, knowing suspicion would fall on the owner. They're pretty matey with each other.'

'Have they been arrested?'

'No, not yet. The vehicle's still missing. The police are searching the bush around Eversleigh They're taking a very serious view of the whole thing, as well they might. First a bomb gets thrown at Hugh, presumably by the logging fraternity, now one of the leaders of said fraternity is run down by members of the Greenies, their traditional enemies. Seems we've got a nice little range war starting here, mister.'

'Hell! I don't want Annie in any danger.'

'We'll hope it doesn't come to that. White's respected by all sides. Why'd they want to pick on him or his people?'

'Tell me, why was Eversleigh catching the train at all?' I'd been puzzled since Duke had told me. 'Why didn't he drive down to Brisbane?'

Duke laughed shortly. 'Apparently he's a bit of a conservationist himself,' he said. 'Doesn't like using his car unnecessarily. Wasting the earth's resources, damage to the ozone layer and all that. Bloody ironic, isn't it?'

Duke agreed to join us for dinner. 'Fran will be there, and Maria,' he said. 'Fran'a helping Luigi out. One of the girls is off sick.'

As I rang off there was a tap on the door and Annie strolled in.

'Am I disturbing you?' She smiled.

'Never.' It was a lie. She was disturbing me a great deal. I gave her Duke's version of the accident.

'That's nasty,' she said thoughtfully.

'You be very careful on Mitchell Island,' I warned her. 'I want you to stay in one piece.'

She looked startled. 'I won't be in any danger. I'll be with the boss. No one's going to involve us. Anyway —' she smiled reassuringly—'how many times have I told you, don't worry about me. I'm a big girl now and I can —'

'I know, I know,' I interrupted, "take care of myself". All the same, I wish I was going with you.'

She was stroking Carnie and looked up. 'Don't fuss,' she reproved me. 'I'll be all right.'

She stayed for a while, chatting, but shying away from any intimacy which crept into the conversation from my side. I had an uncomfortable feeling that I was being assessed in some way and prayed I'd measure up. Eventually she left me to visit with the other tenants and I took myself off to Paddo's 7-to-7 to replenish my groceries—and Carnie's favourite tinned milk. She'd probably fang me in the leg if I ever ran out of the stuff. She was named because of her addiction to it—Carnation Belle Douglas, aristo-

cratic Abyssinian from her nose to her red-gold tail, but
just a scruff at heart, like they all are.

Luigi's is more Italian than Italy, with a big pizza oven
in the front window where Luigi's son Tony tosses pizza
dough into the air for the entertainment of the passers-by
and does magical things with mushroom and mozzarella.
Inside, the tablecloths are red-checked, the walls muralled
with scenes of the sunny Mediterranean and Chianti bottles
hang in cane baskets from the ceiling, vying for space with
rampant plastic grape vines. The food is authentic and
attracts the local Italians. At one table a group of old men
sits most nights, playing cards and drinking wine. It's their
second home, where they can be comfortable in their own
language.

The film crew arrived, having smuggled themselves out
through the back of the hotel. As we greeted each other,
Luigi came bustling between the tables, hands spread wide,
grinning all over his face.

'Eh! Micky, Peta—and the beautiful Annie, you come
home at last, that's-a-good,' he beamed, embracing Annie.
'I find you a nice table, and Fran comes to take your order.'
He winked broadly at the girls and slapped me heartily on
the shoulder. 'You're a lucky fella tonight, eh Micky? You
got two beautiful ladies here.' And he was off to harry his
waiters.

It was a warm, relaxed evening. As we lingered over
gelati and coffee another son produced an accordion and
Luigi's strong, musical tenor filled the room. Francesca
joined us as the patrons thinned, going on to their Saturday
night entertainments, and Maria came out from the kitchen
to climb into her mother's lap, her soft black curls framing
a sweet baby face with pink cheeks and large dark eyes.

'G'day, Micky.' She smiled gently at me and cast me a
limpid look from under her incredibly long lashes. God,
they start early! 'When you coming to see me at mi casa?'

Everyone at the table choked and she looked around
severely. 'What is funny?' she demanded.

'Nothing, bambina,' I assured her, hastily wiping the grin off my face. She slithered down from Francesca and trotted firmly over to me.

'Up!' she commanded, lifting her arms and I settled her in the crook of my own as we shared my gelati.

We chatted back and forth as the evening grew late. Maria slept against my arm, killing my muscles, her little face delicately flushed. Annie described some of their work in Africa and told us how Jansen had filmed a charging elephant.

'He just lay down and let it run over the top of him,' she said, adding tartly to the big Dutchman, 'You might have been killed.'

His crooked grin was warmer for her. 'I wanted the shot and I like elephants,' he said mildly. 'She wouldn't have hurt me. Not so clumsy as they look, elephants. She never touched me. Just to frighten me, I think.'

Well, that's got you stymied, I told him silently, with great satisfaction. Annie can't handle her men getting into dangerous situations. That's why she left me, old mate. You've bloody had it now!

'You're like Duke.' Fran smiled at him. 'He's always running into danger and assuming he'll be all right—and so sorry afterwards and he'll never do it again, of course.'

Duke took her hand. 'Until next time; but she loves me, in spite of it all.'

'How can you stand it?' Annie asked curiously. 'All the worry?'

Fran looked at her, her oval, Botticelli face serene. 'Well, I don't like it, and I do worry, of course,' she said slowly, 'but what's the alternative? If I want Duke, I have to take him as he is. If I tried to make him change, give up his work, settle down, it wouldn't be the same. It would be like taking the essence out of him—like the perfume from a flower or the taste out of the wine. Whatever makes Duke who he is, that's part of it. He wouldn't be Duke otherwise, and it's Duke I want.' She stopped, blushing. 'I'm saying it very badly.'

Duke looked at her and raised her hand to his lips. 'You're saying it beautifully, madonna mia,' he said gently. Annie watched them with—was it fear in her eyes?

Luigi began to sing 'Come Back to Sorrento' and O'Hara opened another bottle of wine. Maria slept on, making a hot, damp patch on my arm.

It was a special night, friendly, gentle, filled with wine and song. I look back now and think of the peace and calm —before the storm broke over our heads, shattering us all.

CHAPTER 8

We walked to the nearby taxi-rank together, down the winding main road. On either side, the sharply sloping streets of Paddington plunge down, leaving houses to fend as best they can, teetering on impossibly high stumps in their steep, multi-terraced back gardens. Lawn-mowers cower in fright at the prospect of actually having to risk the steep grassy slopes and mow the stuff! Every yard was thick with greenery, vines and flowering trees, all sweetly scenting the moonlight.

I fell in beside Grant and asked the question that had been on my mind since the news broadcast.

'Why were you at the back of the house?'

'I heard a noise and went to investigate, thank God!'

'Why at the back, though? Surely the noise would have been at the front. That's where they threw the bomb.'

He grinned up at me, his thick lenses reflecting the street lights.

'I've a valuable collection of fossils and manuscripts I keep in an office out the back. First thought was, someone's trying to get them. It's happened before. I was dozy with sleep and thought, hell, the bloody alarm's not working, so I didn't wait to put on a dressing-gown or slippers. I'd no sooner got out the back when my bedroom was blown to kingdom come!'

'Lucky!' I commented.

To my annoyance, Jansen continued on with us after the others had said their goodnights and been whisked away in their taxis. I'd made the mistake of telling Annie about the possum while she'd been talking to Carnie and she'd told Jansen, of course. He never seemed to be without his camera, and came back to No. 18. Bloody cheek!

'Why's her fur all rufty—she's got scabs!' Annie had looked at me accusingly.

'Her own fault.' I'm all for personal responsibility. It's the compost heap. It's turned out to be a great favourite of our newest neighbour, a pushy, thick-furred, grey and amber brushtail possum. He scavenges there on moony nights, pausing only to beat up next door's cat when it comes prowling.

As we humans cut down the possums' habitat and spread our suburbs, they in turn move right back in, defending their backyard territories with fervour, holding running battles with cats and flying foxes. On these nights the warm, moon-bright air is filled with screeches and howls and the distinctive, rasping cough of angry possum.

'Don't you get involved,' I had cautioned Carnie, and she looked at me with scornful green eyes and escaped through the cat flap in the back door screen. I tried to coax her off the fence but she slid quietly into the shadowed back alley, looking over her shoulder just once, eyes glowing. The next morning her red-gold hair was a little ragged in places and she was sporting a long scratch down her nose. By the compost heap a lone tuft of exquisitely soft grey fur told its own story. Honour was apparently satisfied.

'I'll show you,' I told Jansen helpfully as we entered No. 18. 'We don't want to be all trooping out there. He'll be scared off.' But Annie came too. Peta ran upstairs to get a banana and, instead of properly ignoring the whole business and putting Jansen back in his place, the little beast performed to perfection, climbing head first, hand over hand down the mango tree to daintily take pieces of banana from Annie's fingers. Then he posed on the grass and ate them, oblivious of the camera, and had the hide to follow us back to the house demanding more.

'Greedy little devil,' I complained. 'He's as fat as he can stand already! Who's for coffee?'

We all were, Peta doing the honours this time. Of course, Jansen managed to get himself on the sofa next to Annie.

'We were able to do another interview this afternoon,' Annie said, 'with Ted Miles, Sinclair Faraday's right hand man. Faraday's head forester on Mitchell Island. Ted was in Brisbane for the weekend so he came around. He's an interesting man. Seems very knowledgeable about forests. He hates all this fuss. Says it reflects on the foresters.'

'How come?' I asked.

'Well, he says Faraday's been a forester for ten years and spent five years training. He's got a degree in science, he really cares about the forest and his staff is equally well trained and dedicated. He studied in Europe and he knows all the different types of forest, world wide. Ted says this is harming their credibility as professionals and that, while he understands the conservationists' point of view, they're far too emotive about what they see as damage. He says the foresters have their reputation and they're proud of their work.'

'That's right,' Jansen agreed. 'Apparently there is a lot of confusion about what sort of forest is on Mitchell Island anyway. The foresters say it is eucalypt forest with a rainforest understorey.'

'They call it "transition forest",' Annie added. 'But a CSIRO expert who was consulted when the land sale was being negotiated calls it "wet scleriphyll".' Her brow wrinkled as she pronounced it carefully.

'Come again?' I protested.

'Tall eucalypts and the ground storey of softwood species with palms. He says it's not rainforest at all.'

Jansen nodded. 'But if you take Hugh Grant's opinion, it's *because* of the palms and lianas and brush box and satinay that it is a true rainforest. So they are all very different. The row is over logging rainforest. So, if you accept the scientists' point of view, then none at all is being logged. Accept the conservationists' ideas and large areas of rainforest are being logged.'

Annie put down her cup. 'The Government supported the scientists' report when Hugh took them to court but public opinion was against cutting down any more trees, whatever category, so he had a lot of sympathy on his side. These days, public opinion is changing the world.'

'Grant says as long as the people are caught up in the emotional issue of logging rainforest, the Government Inquiry won't go against the World Heritage Listing,' Jansen said. He sounded pleased. It was clear where his sympathies lay. How could he be a wild man of the woods if they chopped down the woods he depended on for his photos?

I brought him back to reality. You sometimes have to be cruel to be kind. 'Public opinion's notoriously fickle,' I told him. 'Give them an equally good reason to log the island and watch the people then.'

'Cynic!' was all I got from Annie and Peta in unison and a quizzical look from the Dutchman.

Annie walked Jansen to the front door. I went with them and thankfully saw him off the premises.

'He's nice, isn't he?' Annie said. 'I'm glad you like him too.'

And they're supposed to have all this insight! At Peta's door she turned awkwardly to me.

'Micky, I'll be busy most of tomorrow and then we transfer to Mitchell on Monday. It doesn't give us much time to talk and I think we need to.'

'Yes.' My mouth was dry. 'You've been a long time coming home, love.'

'Things have changed,' she said baldly. 'I've changed. I've been living in a much bigger world, more exciting. It's very addictive. I want to stay there and explore it for a while yet. And —' she hesitated, looking up at me imploringly— 'I'm not sure about my feelings any more. Once I was so certain what I wanted. I was about to write and say I'd come home and we could try it again, and then—the boss came along and—and Hank.'

I swallowed. I can put two and two together and come up with five like anyone else.

'I suppose it's Jansen,' I said, not wanting to hear the answer.

'I don't know,' she said miserably. 'I like him a lot—I think I love him. I know he loves me—but there's you, and I do love you, Micky.' She stopped, looking so unhappy I folded her into my arms for comfort. From somewhere in my chest I heard a small, 'I'm so confused.'

I chuckled. Although I was hurting for her and hurting for me, it was a ridiculous situation and I suddenly saw the humour in it.

'Take your time, love,' I advised her gently, elated at holding her like old times. 'I haven't changed, I still want you, and I'll be here whenever you need me. I can't help you decide, but I promise you I'll give Jansen a run for his money. He won't walk off with my girl so easily.'

She looked up anxiously, then smiled, suddenly mischievous. 'That's too mediæval for words. Micky, I'll make time to see you, when this assignment's over. I'm due a holiday. Wait till I get back from the island and we'll spend a few days together, OK?'

'Heaven,' I assured her and kissed her cheek, then thought, bugger nobility! and transferred to her mouth. She didn't pull away. Stick that in your portfolio, Jansen!

I hardly saw her the next day, only briefly after dinner, and half the crew were at Peta's. Early Monday morning we took them to the station and they caught the Eversleigh train. I felt depressed. My Annie being carried off into God knew what situation—and with Hank Bloody Jansen for company!

CHAPTER 9

Duke dropped in for lunch on Monday.

'Heard the news?'

'What particular news would that be?' I inquired.

'On the radio this morning.'

'I didn't have time to listen. I was getting Annie and Co. to the train.'

He grinned. 'There's been a positive ID of the two Greenies. It was them all right!'

'Oh?' My mind was on other things.

Duke snapped his fingers under my nose. 'Wake up, mate! The police put them in a line-up and the bloke who'd given the most detailed description picked them out, no hesitation. They've been charged with attempted murder.'

I pulled my mind away from Annie and Jansen and made an effort to appear interested. 'I suppose they've admitted it all, now?'

'Not a bit of it. Still swearing they were nowhere near their vehicle or the railway station. The Land-Rover's still not found. Police've looked everywhere.'

'They can't have looked everywhere,' I commented drily. 'They haven't looked where it is.'

'Ha-ha, who's a clever dick? They'll find it. There's a heap of countryside around Eversleigh. Anyway, while it's all very interesting it doesn't get me any forrarder on who chucked a bomb at old Hughie.'

'How are you tackling it?'

'It's not easy. Even if someone saw the warning letter being posted—and how'd you know who was posting what? —no one in Eversleigh would say and dob in a fellow citizen. They're all under threat, as they see it, and most of them would only be too happy to have Grant stopped.'

'Who are your favourites for the job?'

Duke wrinkled his nose and drummed his fingers restlessly on the chair arm. 'Well, there's the Eversleighs themselves. The mill would be forced to close if the logging
was stopped—and it was Brent Eversleigh who copped the
retaliation. Suppose someone in MICO knows more than
he or she is letting on? Hugh's president of MICO, he
founded it. This hit-and-run pair, Barbara Deakin and
Jeremy Hall, might have decided to mete out justice.'

'True. Who else?'

'Sinclair Faraday comes up next in my book. He's made
no secret of his annoyance over the proposed World Heritage listing and he's diametrically opposed to Hugh on all
issues.'

'Except that he cares about the forest and uses the sustainable yield system to protect it.'

'Every bloody person involved says he cares about the
forest! They're all pushing their own cases and bad-
mouthing the opposition! Faraday's reputation is being damaged and he's a professional man with a fairly short fuse.'

'It wouldn't mean his job, though,' I objected. 'He works
for the Forestry Department. His team would simply be
moved to a new location if logging was stopped on
Mitchell.'

'He's pretty angry. Seems to think it's his forest and he
knows best how to look after it. However, if you don't fancy
him, try Les Brown. He's the logging contractor, the man
behind the buzz saw. He employs a team of blokes who
have families to support, are always being held up as the
villains whenever the forest issue raises its fuzzy green head,
and he's a local, as are all his men. They wouldn't be too
thrilled to have to up camp and go to other timber areas.
They've got kids in school there, mates in the town, their
wives are involved in the local social scene.'

'Sounds a prospect. Anyone else?'

'That's just the short list. Add 397 other angry residents,
all terrified this'll mean the end of Eversleigh—then
there're the outsiders.'

'Namely?'

'Namely anyone with the urge to make trouble or with a grudge against Hugh. You know, White made an interesting point the other night. Outside interests.'

'To stop the Government Inquiry?' I asked, remembering back.

'To *influence* it, more like. Look! Mitchell Island is an extremely hot potato for the Government. Supposing someone wanted to take advantage of the situation to keep it on the boil?'

'Why?' I'm sometimes painfully innocent. Duke told me why. Thinking of Annie over there on the island I was less than happy. Duke read my mind.

'She'll be OK,' he said positively. 'No one's going to involve Damien White or his people. That'd make the potato far too hot to handle.'

I prayed he was right. Next day, events proved him dead wrong—no pun intended.

Tuesday rose, warm and scented with a thousand spring blossoms stretching their petals after being locked up for the winter. In the park over the road, bees were buzzing ecstatically in the jacaranda trees which carpeted the grass with flowers so intensely blue they defied the eyes to absorb it. My heart responded, in spite of itself, and I began to hum along with nature as Carnie and I went for a morning stroll around the back yard, stopping to watch fellow tenant Al Wang revolving gracefully and with absorbed concentration under the mango tree, doing his daily tai-chi.

In the middle of breakfast, Duke rang.

'Well, I got no joy there,' he complained. 'It seems there are no dark plans afoot to re-open the submission for a tourist development on Mitchell Island. The original companies, Wilson Properties and the Nishida Land Company, have gone their separate ways. Dan Nishida is busy buying up hotels on the Gold Coast, Wilson's gone back to building town house complexes in suburbia.'

I sympathized.

'Oh well, it was a reasonable assumption,' he said, reluctant to let it go. 'The Government might have been happy to sell Mitchell to developers if it had grown too big a problem, but no one's expressing interest that I can see. I think I'll take a drive up to Eversleigh.'

I washed the breakfast things, wondering how on earth I was going to occupy myself that day and all the days until Annie was through with this job. As I wiped down the draining-board the phone rang again.

Bugger Duke! I thought crossly. I don't give a damn what he's found out about the bloody island. If I never hear about Mitchell Island again, it'll be too soon!

The long distance pips sounded and I held my breath as Annie came through, sounding definitely anxious.

'Micky? Micky? Thank goodness! I rang a while back but you were engaged.'

'Duke,' I said briefly. 'You sound all of a tizz, love. Are you OK?'

'No,' she said, and her voice was strained. 'Not OK. Oh, Micky, Melody Scott. She's dead!'

'Eh?' I was startled. 'Good God, love, how?'

'It was an accident,' she said miserably. 'She went for a walk last evening and didn't come back. They found her this morning. She'd slipped and hit her head on a rock and fallen into some water. She drowned.' Her voice filled with tears. 'Poor Melody. It's horrible!'

'Oh, Annie!' I wanted desperately to be with her, to comfort her. 'Poor darling.'

She pulled herself together and said shakily, 'The boss wants to talk to you. We've been having an emergency meeting. Here he is.' There was the noise of movement on the line, then White's BBC announcer's voice.

'Mr Douglas? Annie has told you of our predicament. We're all very distressed but have voted to continue our project. The thing is, we need a scriptwriter. Annie thought you might do the job.'

'I've no experience,' I told him. 'I write children's books.'

'It's not so very different, I suspect,' he said. 'I need someone with a gift of words who can describe a scene and tell a good story. I always do the final draft myself, and we'd give you all the help we can. O'Hara knows his way around a script, but he's only back-up and we need him for other things.'

'Gofer!' I heard O'Hara yell in the background. 'Tea-boy and dogsbody!'

'The thing is, we're on a strictly limited schedule and to find someone else might take longer than we have. Will you do it?'

I thought fast. I wasn't tied up with a book at the moment, Alan, my publisher, wasn't breathing fire and brimstone about deadlines, my life was my own and free of commitment for the time being. And I'd be on the island with Annie, putting a spoke in Jansen's wheel. I heard myself agreeing.

'I'll give it a go. Put Annie back on, please.'

Annie took the receiver. 'Thanks, Micky. I know you can handle it.'

'I'll do my best,' I promised. 'Is there anything you want me to bring you, love?'

We arranged for me to catch the two o'clock ferry, which meant a hasty packing, boarding Carnie with Monica and a fast drive to Eversleigh. A stop-off at the Parks & Wildlife Office for my permit to cross to the Island—you can't go over without one—and I made it in the nick of time, parking in the ferry car park—it was four-wheel drive only on Mitchell—and sprinting down to the jetty where the *Island Queen* was doing her thing, coming slowly forward to drift against the line of old tyres lashed to the pier. A sign along the wheelhouse proclaimed 'Lowe's Island Tours'. A grinning deck-hand, no more than sixteen and dark-tanned, with ragged jeans and a Jackie Howe singlet, slung ropes to shore. I hastily bought my ticket at a small building, not much bigger than a cupboard, and carried my cases down the pier, scanning the waiting vehicles and passengers.

The afternoon air was being pleasantly cooled by a light, salty breeze from the east and a small flock of hopeful sea-gulls cruised above the jetty, calling harshly to one another. There seemed to be a lot of people crossing to the island.

A small knot of men stood apart, one tall, mid-forties, with a thatch of bright red hair, slightly grizzled at the temples. With him were a slim, dark youth, casually dressed, with film star good looks and a cat-like elegance, and an older man, grey-haired, in a sober suit. Two others, one thin and sad-faced with sparse blonde hair and the other fair-skinned and smiling with tight, sandy curls, completed the group. They had a small heap of luggage, as well as official-looking briefcases and camera equipment. My heart sank as I watched the red-haired man giving instructions. I could only think of one reason why Detective-Inspector David Reeves and his team from Brisbane Homicide should be catching the ferry to Mitchell Island, and the thought was not my favourite for the day.

CHAPTER 10

Reeves didn't look particularly surprised to see me.

'I heard Miss Mason is involved,' he observed. 'I supposed you'd be around somewhere.'

We stood at the rail on the passenger deck, high above the sardined vehicles, watching Eversleigh dwindling across the stretch of calm sea which isolated the island. In the distance crested terns in flocks of hundreds wheeled over the channel, bright eyes watching for fish shoals.

'I take it you're here because of Melody Scott,' I finished, 'but Annie told me it was an accident.'

He looked down, seemingly absorbed by the smooth cobalt water swirling against the ferry's side, then cast a quick glance around. The only people in earshot were the stolid Sergeant Hobbs and his companion, Sergeant Harry Andrews, otherwise known as Handsome Harry of Homicide, and nowhere near as young as he looked. Beside them Reeves's technical officers, the sandy-haired Scot, Iain McBride, and the sad-faced Les Sheppard, watched Mitchell Island approaching, tall and heavy with forest.

'We don't think it was an accident,' Reeves said softly. 'Autopsy revealed an interesting anomaly. Odd abrasions on her body and, although she was found in a fresh-water pool, the water in her lungs was salt.'

'Hell! Then Duke was wrong.'

He looked interested. 'Duke Jordan? Your journalist friend? Where does he come in?'

I told him of Grant's request to Duke and of Duke's calm assurance that no one would involve Damien White's team in the row over the island.

'You think it's to do with the conflict over the logging?'

'Can you think of a better reason? It looks to me as if the loggers, or someone to do with the timber industry,

organized Grant's bomb, MICO took its revenge on Brent
Eversleigh, and now someone in the opposition camp has
decided to make it so hot for White that he'll abandon his
documentary, which is seen to be siding with the Green
movement, whatever his assurances of totally fair and
unbiased reporting.' I indicated a newspaper, abandoned
on a seat by a former passenger. It was the *Eversleigh Sun*,
and the headlines asked boldly, IS WHITE REALLY
GREEN? 'It looks obvious to me,' I finished.

'Well, as a hard-working copper, I'm not supposed to
jump to the obvious,' David said sardonically.'I have to make
a show of detection at least, and it's amazing how often the
obvious can be wrong. But Micky —' he looked at me from
under his bushy red brows, suddenly stern—'I'll find out the
truth, and you work on your film script and don't go
detecting on your own for Miss Mason's sake.'

I shrugged. As if I would! 'Absolutely.' I nodded.
Andrews smiled widely in the background and winked at
Hobbs. Disbelieving sod!

We idled and throbbed to the Mitchell Island jetty. A
small flock of pelicans rode the water and black-and-white
oyster catchers ran anxiously about on the beach, dodg-
ing the waves, fishing for pippy shells. Out of reach of the
water the sand was pock-marked with little breathing holes
where the shells lurked under the surface. Annie was waiting as we tied up. For once Jansen was nowhere in sight.
A smart young uniformed constable met the detectives and
shepherded them off on foot down a narrow sand road
which led to a cluster of buildings set against a tangle of
low green palms and scrubby undergrowth. The shore was
a long curve of wide white beach which rose to low sand
dunes sporting silver trails of beach spinifex and low twisted
banksias and wattles, fighting for a scrubby existence with
casuarinas. These gave way to higher, wooded hills and,
still moving upwards, to the thick dark green forest, standing tall against the sky on the massive dunes of the interior.
A sweet scent of eucalypt was in the air, mingling with the

tang of salt breeze. I breathed the freshness deeply as I made my way to Annie, who was standing tautly a little way off.

She smiled with relief and made a quick movement towards me as if she was about to fling herself into my arms. I half raised them, then dropped them awkwardly to my side as she restrained herself. She was pale, in spite of her African tan, and her eyes were dark and blue-shadowed.

'My poor love!' I said, concerned.

'It's awful!' she said in a low voice that I had to strain to hear. 'They say it's murder—and that was Inspector Reeves, wasn't it?'

'It was, love. Don't worry. He'll sort it out and get who-ever did it.'

'We've already had that young constable asking us all sorts of questions—if any of us had anything against Melody, if we'd quarrelled with her, who'd seen her leave, did everyone have an alibi. As if we'd done it!' Her voice rose indignantly. 'Isn't it just part of this whole stupid business about the logging?'

'It looks like it to me, but the police have to cover every possible angle,' I soothed. 'It's just routine, love. No one believed either side would be stupid enough to attack White's people and create such an international stink, so they have to look for all other possibilities.'

'Well, I put him straight!' she fumed. 'I told him in no uncertain terms what I thought of his questions and that Melody was a lovely girl. We all liked her enormously. She was kind and helpful and made everything run so smoothly.' She gulped and I took her arm for comfort. 'I've taken over all the organizational work she did—you'll only have the script to worry about and Paddy and the boss will show you what we need.' She stopped and looked at me accusingly. 'How come this sort of thing happens when you're around?'

In spite of her obvious distress, I was annoyed. Did I ask them to come and make their documentary and get mixed up with a hornets' nest? No, I bloody didn't. I explained this to her as she led me to a macho Land-Cruiser with crossed palm trees painted on the door.

'I'm sorry, Micky,' she sighed as I heaved my case on to the back seat and deposited my portable typewriter more gently beside it. 'You're right, of course. It's just—you seem to attract trouble.'

She turned the wheel expertly and we bounced off in the direction that the detectives had taken. Mitchell Village consisted of a two-storey pub from the last century with fancy white lace ironwork festooning the long balconies, making it look like an ornate wedding cake—named, appropriately, Mitchell Hotel, a general store, souvenir shop, a butchery grandly displaying the name 'Mitchell Meat Hall', a small bait and fishing tackle shop, a garage, Mitchell Motors, and, surprisingly, a second-hand bookshop.

The buildings were all neat and well kept, with clean paintwork and contrasting trims. Palms were in profusion, making a bright, tropical atmosphere and the afternoon sun poured its golden light over the scene.

'The resorts get their supplies from the mainland and have their own tourist trap shops,' Annie explained as we turned off the main road to follow a rutted, sandy track, 'so the village caters mostly for locals and day trippers. Sue Murray tells us there are a couple of good restaurants too, behind the main shops. A Chinese place which does take-aways and a steak house and grill. And the pub does meals as well, so the campers and backpackers can have a break from camp cooking.'

I'd seen David Reeves and the young constable at the door of the pub so I supposed the Brisbane detectives were putting up there.

'They'd have to,' Annie agreed. 'I gather it's the only accommodation other than the resorts. Sue says there's no police station, though she thinks there should be with all the tourists who come. The island is policed from the mainland.'

We lurched slowly along on our low pressured tyres, essential for the deep sand, heading back to the west, land-ward side of the island, although at a tangent.

'Paradise Palms is on the shore a few kilometres from the jetty,' Annie explained, 'but vehicles are forbidden to drive on the beach. Apparently they used to but someone sun-bathing was struck by a beach buggy and killed, so all beach vehicles were banned.'

And a good thing, too. You should be able to enjoy a quiet sunbathe without giving your life for it!

The trees ahead suddenly thinned and our track breasted a series of low dunes and ran up to a long, single-storey building with wide, shady verandahs. Nearby, folk splashed about in a blue-tiled swimming pool while others lounged in deckchairs. Tables under wide yellow-striped beach umbrellas held tall, frosty drinks. A young man in a colour-ful shirt darted about with a tray, gathering up used glasses and delivering refills. To the right and left, backing on to shallow, sparsely wooded dunes, were small, neat cabins, six each side.

Annie pulled up outside the main building. As I got down from the Rover sand clung to my shoes, although around the resort it had been mixed with wood chips to give it some stability. I followed her inside. To the left off the entrance hall was a small office where a woman in her late thirties sat writing at a large desk. She was dressed in bright green cotton trousers and a multi-coloured blouse and her dark gold hair was confined in a neat plait around her head. She looked up and gave a friendly smile as we entered. Over-head a ceiling fan clicked lazily around, stirring the warm air.

'Sue, this is Michael Douglas,' Annie introduced me. 'Micky, Sue Murray.'

She put out her hand and her smile deepened. 'You're very welcome, Mr Douglas.'

'Micky,' I told her, and signed the register which lay open on her desk. She turned to Annie.

'I had a phone call from a Detective-Inspector Reeves,' she said. 'He's coming over to interview everyone at four o'clock. I've told Mr White. This is a dreadful business, really dreadful.' She looked sober. 'There's never been any trouble of this kind before—no real violence. Any protests have been quite peaceful. Certainly no one's been *murdered*!'

'Does anyone have any idea what happened?' I asked Annie as we walked towards the bungalows which clustered together under a stand of eucalypts to the right of the main house.

'Not a clue,' she told me. 'We arrived on the morning ferry around ten a.m. and settled in. Then we talked to Sue and filmed an interview with her and got an overall view of the island way of life. We did some more filming for background—the shore and looking across to Eversleigh— and went for a walk in the bush, except on this side of the island it's all very scrubby. The real wilderness is on the surf side, across the island, and inland. We drew up schedules of our filming and who we needed to interview on the island then it was dinner-time. We talked with the other guests after dinner, then the boys got up a card game. Just before I turned in, at about nine-thirty, Melody said she'd like to take a walk along the beach, beyond where we'd filmed. She's in the habit of taking a stroll before bed wherever we are, and can be gone for an hour or more. She likes—liked —to go alone. I think she worked out scripts in her head as she walked.' I nodded. I'm much the same when I'm working out a book.

'And she didn't come back?'

Annie shook her head miserably. 'I'm feeling very much to blame,' she suddenly blurted out. 'You see, we're all in twin share cabins and of course, being the only girls, I was sharing with Melody. I went to bed with a book but I was so tired, I didn't wait up for her. I switched off the light at ten o'clock. I assumed she'd be back any time. She often stayed up late—a real night owl! I slept like a log. Didn't stir until six o'clock this morning, when the cockatoos started up. A flock of them roosts in a nearby tree and they make a racket every morning, apparently. Melody's bed hadn't been slept in. Then I raised the alarm. If only I'd stayed awake longer I might have realized she was an awfully long time coming in.'

She began to cry and I put my arm around her. There didn't seem to be anything I could say which would comfort her, so I just stood there while she gave way to her grief and wept bitterly against my chest.

CHAPTER 11

'Now let me get this straight.' Reeves smiled around at his audience. 'You're in these three bungalows nearest to the main house. Mr White and Mr Edgely in this closest one, Miss Mason and Miss Scott in the middle and Mr Jansen and Mr O'Hara in the third one.'

White nodded. We were gathered in the cabin he shared with Edgely which was scrupulously tidy, with bright floral curtains and matching bedspreads, light cane furniture and a bare, highly polished wooden floor. There was a woven grass mat beside each bed. The bungalows were identically furnished, differing only in the floral prints of the curtains and covers. Each had a wide verandah at the front with a cane table and two comfortable chairs. I'd been fixed up with a camp bed in the third cabin, with O'Hara and, of course, Jansen. It suited me. He couldn't get up to much with Annie under my unswerving eye.

When I'd arrived, the team members had been trying to occupy themselves with their normal routine. Jansen was closeted in the fourth bungalow which he'd turned into his workroom and a darkroom for developing his film. He was editing the interview with Sue Murray, filmed the previous day, and didn't appear until the Inspector arrived. He'd greeted me quietly and seemed preoccupied and withdrawn. Edgely had been in the nearby bush taping the sounds of the island, which rang with bird calls—the drawn-out crack of the whip bird, the screeches of wild cockatoos, the genial laughter of a flock of kookaburras. White and O'Hara, working on their schedules, had greeted me almost with relief and had begun at once to brief me on the script, while Annie sat silently, her thoughts elsewhere.

I looked around the group. They were all subdued, watching David, still with traces of shock in their eyes.

Sergeant Hobbs sat in a corner, unobtrusively taking notes. Andrews was in Annie's cabin, giving it the once over, though what he hoped to find was beyond me.

'I want to make one thing clear,' the Inspector told them quietly. 'Your colleague, Miss Scott, did not meet her death by accident. You were, I expect, hoping that we were wrong in thinking it was murder, but I assure you, that is not so. We'd be grateful for your total cooperation, no matter how unreasonable our questions may appear to you.'

Annie flushed and hung her head. She was sitting between Jansen and me. Mr White looked steadily at Reeves.

'I'm sure I speak for us all, Inspector. We'll do anything we can to help, naturally. Constable Graham has already taken our statements and the truth is, none of us knows anything at all. Poor Melody went for her usual evening walk and didn't come back. That's really all we can tell you.'

Reeves nodded in his calm way. 'I realize you've already been through this, but I'd like to hear it first hand, if I may, so if you wouldn't mind . . .' He shifted the notes in his lap and the crew members made various noises to indicate their willingness.

'Miss Mason, as you shared a cabin with Miss Scott and reported her missing, perhaps you'll begin. Just tell me about last night.'

Annie told her story again. Reeves listened intently. 'And you say she was going to walk on the beach?' he asked, consulting his notes.

'There's a sort of point up the beach to the north, further than we'd filmed. She wanted to see what was beyond it. As far as I know, that's what she planned to do.'

'Surely she wouldn't have seen much at night?'

'There was a bright moon,' Annie said. 'It was a very clear night.'

'So there was,' Reeves agreed. 'And she didn't say any-

thing to make you think she'd changed her mind and meant
to strike inland?'

'Nothing at all.'

'You see, I think you're all aware that Miss Scott's body
was found about an hour's walk from the resort, not on the
beach, but in the hills behind. Now, either she changed her
mind and walked in that direction, or she was taken there
by another person, perhaps after she was dead.'

Jansen looked annoyed as Annie gave a little gasp and
sniffed into her damp handkerchief. 'Yes, we are all aware
of this, Inspector. I think we understand the implications.'

'I'm sorry to have to spell it out again, and I do realize
how upsetting this must be. The thing is, we can't wait for
you to recover from your shock. That would waste valuable
time and perhaps allow a murderer to go free.'

Jansen subsided and patted Annie's hand. Reeves looked
mildly at him.

'What about your own movements last night, Mr
Jansen?'

Jansen eyed the Inspector for a moment, then shrugged.
'I was playing cards with Paddy and Craig when Annie
went to bed. The girls left for their cabin together. Melody
said something about going for a walk—I didn't take much
notice, I must admit. It was her usual routine, as Annie
has told you. She mentioned that it was getting chilly and
she would go back with Annie for a cardigan and —'

David interrupted. 'There's nothing about that in the
constable's notes.'

Jansen looked quickly at Annie. 'Well, as I said, I wasn't
attending especially. I could have been wrong.'

Annie gulped miserably. 'No, no—you were right. I'm
sorry, Inspector, I completely forgot. The shock, I expect.
Of course, Melody walked back to the cabin with me and
put on a cardigan. There was quite a cool breeze getting
up.'

'Can you describe this cardigan, Miss Mason?'

Annie looked surprised. 'Well, it was the one she must

have been wearing when you—when she was found. Pink wool with a little ribbed pattern—and pink pearl buttons.'

'I see, yes. Thank you, Miss Mason. Please go on, Mr Jansen.'

'Well, as I said, we were playing cards. That was in the main building, of course, in the lounge. The girls went out. I didn't look at the time, but I'm told it was nine-thirty. We continued playing for an hour, then Miss Murray offered us coffee and we had supper. They look after you very well here.'

'Do you remember where Mr White was while you were playing cards?'

'Eh? Oh, he was reading for a while, a little apart from us. Miss Murray has some excellent books about the area in the pioneering days. I believe it was one of those. When we finished playing, he was not there—but I couldn't say what time he left. There were various other guests in the lounge, so I'm sure one of them will have been sharper eyed than me, but —' he smiled ironically—'I'm sure he will tell you himself.'

Craig Edgely stirred but caught David's eye and remained silent.

'And after supper?'

'Well, that would be at about eleven o'clock. The boss said we should turn in as we had a busy day ahead of us.'

Reeves interrupted again. 'So Mr White was with you after supper?'

'Oh yes, Inspector, he came back in at ten-thirty as Miss Murray was pouring the coffee.'

Damien White had sat silently during this exchange, watching David with interest, as if studying the habits of a new and interesting species. David looked at him with a decided twinkle, and turned again to Jansen.

'Right! Go on, Mr Jansen.'

The big Dutchman stroked his beard reflectively. 'There's nothing more. Paddy and I walked to our bunga-low. I went straight to bed. Paddy is a cigar-smoker and went outside to smoke one of the filthy things. This ensures harmony between us.' He flashed his crooked grin at the Irishman who winked back, a gleam of humour in his dark eyes.

'Did you hear Mr O'Hara come to bed?'

'No, I think not. I fell asleep almost at once and I'm a sound sleeper. That's all I can tell you, Inspector.'

David nodded and turned to Edgely. 'You wanted to say something, Mr Edgely?'

'Thank you, Inspector, just one point. Everything Hank has told you is correct, except that I saw when Mr White left. He put down his book just after the girls went out and took out his pipe. I looked up and he indicated that he was going outside to smoke it. He left in about five minutes, after he'd filled it.' He looked at White. 'That's right, Damien, isn't it?'

White nodded. 'I didn't look at the time myself. I must have followed the girls about five minutes after they left, perhaps less, but certainly not more.'

'And where did you go, Mr White?' Reeves made a note on one of his sheets.

'I walked down to the beach.' The ecologist smiled. 'Like Paddy, I like to keep the peace as far as smoking is concerned, so I light up outside. There's so much publicity given these days to passive smoking, and not everyone appreciates the smell of a pipe.'

I rather like it myself, but I didn't say so. I felt in a curious position—an outsider, and yet one of the team. Reeves smiled in his quiet way and continued his gentle probing.

'Did you see Miss Scott going for her walk?'

'Yes, I did, as I told the constable. She had already begun to walk along the beach to the north, but wasn't close enough to speak to. I could see her quite clearly in the moonlight. She wouldn't have seen me. I remained directly in front of the main building. There's a path down to the beach and chairs above the tide mark, so I sat there and smoked and watched the water lapping on the sand. It was

all very peaceful.' He looked sad. 'There was I, enjoying
the moonlight and a night bird—a mopoke, and watching
a boat out there on the silver water, with no thought that
poor Melody could be in danger.'

'How could you know?' Reeves said politely. 'And you
didn't see anyone else?'

'On the beach, not a soul, Inspector. There was some
movement around the cabins as people went back and forth
from the main house. I spent quite a while just sitting, as
they say. I returned to the house just as Miss Murray was
serving supper. The rest you know.'

'Not quite,' David countered. 'What did you do after
supper, Mr White?'

'Craig and I came back here and turned in,' he said
simply.

Edgely nodded. 'That's correct, Inspector.'

'And when you'd all retired to your cabins, you didn't
hear any sound, any calls, for instance?'

They all shook their heads, watching each other. Reeves
looked across at O'Hara.

'How long were you smoking your cigar on the verandah?
I assume you stayed there and didn't go for a walk
yourself?'

'No, me dear Inspector, I did not. I smoked and worked
out in me head a piece of recording I'd a mind to suggest
to Craig, and didn't put me foot one inch off the verandah;
although there's no one to be verifying me story, so you'll
have to take me word for it. I'm an honest fellow, as they'll
all be telling you, and with no reason at all to be hurtin'
poor little Melody. I was in me bed and sound asleep by
eleven-thirty, I'd reckon.'

There was a silence tinged with tension as Reeves flicked
through his papers. All eyes were on him, waiting for his
next move. He looked up at last, smiled and stood up.

'Thank you all for your patience. We'll keep out of your
way as much as possible but you'll have to be prepared to

have us asking more questions in due course, as the need arises.'

Everyone murmured something and the relief in the room was tangible. Reeves nodded to Sergeant Hobbs and they went out.

'Well!' Edgely said, and would have continued, but White stood up quickly.

'We've all got work to do,' he said crisply. 'Take our minds off all of this. Is that film ready for us to see, Hank?'

'Oh, sure.' Jansen stretched and smiled down at Annie. 'I'll set it up now.'

I hesitated. 'Do you need me for the moment, Mr White?'

White glanced at the door, then back to me. 'Not immediately, Mr Douglas. Meet us in the fourth cabin when you can.'

A shrewd man, Damien White. 'Thanks,' I said, 'and the name's Micky—boss.'

CHAPTER 12

As I left White's bungalow, Andrews, Sheppard and McBride came out of the fourth cabin along and joined the others.

'Any luck?' Reeves queried and Andrews shook his head.

They've been searching all the cabins, I thought with a shock. No doubt looking for evidence that one of the crew followed Melody Scott last night and drowned her, then dragged her body into the bush.

David turned as I came towards him. 'Micky! Aren't you supposed to be working?'

'In a minute. I want a word with you, David.'

'All right. Walk down to the beach with us.'

Sheppard and McBride waited with their equipment as Reeves and I walked ahead of the two sergeants, following the path White must have taken from the main building to the beach.

'Was that really necessary?' I asked.

'Of course, or I wouldn't have subjected them to it. And just as well. Miss Mason remembered the cardigan. Neither she nor Jansen had mentioned it previously. Shock can blank out whole chunks of memory and important details quite innocently get missed out.'

'I don't see what was so important about a cardigan,' I protested. 'And Annie was thoroughly upset again.'

'Hmmm!' David smiled suddenly. 'God save us from all lovers! The cardigan was very important, Micky, because Miss Scott was not wearing a cardigan when she was found. Neither was any such garment discovered in the area.'

I was silenced. 'I'm sorry, David.'

He stopped and faced me. 'Micky, I understand your— partisan attitude, but for God's sake don't let it get in the way of your intelligence. We don't do this for fun; I don't enjoy making already stressed people go over their stories again. Do have the sense to realize we know what we're doing!'

I swallowed and felt my face reddening. 'You're right, David, I won't bother you again.'

'Chance'd be a fine thing,' he said, casting up his eyes. We'd stopped by a group of half a dozen plastic chairs high on the beach. He indicated them to his men. 'Brian, this will be where Damien White smoked his pipe. We'll have a cast around—perhaps he knocked out the dottle into the sand. Now, what can we see from here?'

We all looked to the north. The beach ran wide and straight until, in the far distance, it disappeared around a jutting headland.

'Twenty minutes' walk?' Reeves asked no one in particular.

'Less,' Harry Andrews objected. 'I could do it in fifteen, probably.'

'But you're an athletic type,' Reeves said pensively. 'For a normal person, say?'

'All right, sir, twenty minutes.'

Reeves grinned at him. 'Well, let's get to work here and then hope we can do it in fifteen. It looks like rain on the way. Now, we have White sitting here, watching Miss Scott and a boat. Unfortunately there are footprints galore. The tide doesn't get up this high, so there's no way of isolating his. Miss Scott would have left her cabin maybe five minutes before he arrived and probably went directly down to the beach, so she'd have come out, what, about fifty metres along from here? Assuming she was walking at an average pace, that would put her still clearly visible in the moonlight but too far away to call out to.'

Hobbs cleared his throat. 'You've only got White's word for it that he was here and she was there,' he said, and Reeves nodded.

'We've got three of them without an alibi,' he agreed. 'Miss Mason—shut up, Micky!—says she went to bed, read for half an hour, then put out the light and went to sleep; White was by himself for a good fifty minutes, and Paddy O'Hara was out of sight after eleven p.m., and we only have his word for it that he went to bed at eleven-thirty. No, Micky, I don't suspect any of them, but no one, even the famous Mr White, is immune from needing an alibi in a murder case.'

Hobbs rubbed his chin thoughtfully. 'That's very true,' he said, 'but we can check Mr White's story by the boat he saw. It won't be difficult to find which boats were out in the passage at that time. Probably a pleasure cruise in the moonlight, or a fishing trawler.'

'Or a private yacht taking advantage of the clear conditions,' Reeves added. 'Get on to it, Brian. Miss Murray may know what boats would be out at that hour—and see if Mr White can describe the vessel.'

Andrews, who'd been searching the sand around the chairs, cast a quick look at his chief. 'It doesn't prove he was here, though,' he said. 'He could have seen the boat from any point on the beach. Hang on!' He'd resumed his careful sifting. 'Here, sir, he knocked his pipe out right here.'

'That's a good sign, if he didn't do it deliberately to give himself an alibi,' Hobbs grunted, coming to join Harry. 'He could have followed Miss Scott, killed her, then made sure he came back here and left his evidence.'

'True,' Reeves nodded. 'What a suspicious mind you have, Brian. Micky, what are you still doing here?'

I couldn't say. I just wanted to know what they were thinking. 'David, will you at least keep me informed?' I blurted out. He looked at me for a minute.

'If you can keep anything I tell you to yourself, as far as I feel able, I'll fill you in as we go,' he said at last. 'I think I can trust you that far.'

'Thanks!' I said heavily.

'You're too one-eyed about Miss Mason,' he said seriously, 'and it's bound to upset your judgement. Come over to the pub tonight, if you like, and have a beer with us.'

'OK.' I grimaced at a sudden thought. 'But I won't be able to help you, David, not as your man on the inside or anything. Not with Annie involved.'

'How little you know me,' he said gently. 'I wouldn't ask it, of course. However, I do know you and I don't think, if you did hear anything incriminating, that you could keep it to yourself. You always need to know the truth—and you've got a strong streak of justice, in case you didn't realize.'

He was right, blast him. I agreed to meet him at the Mitchell Hotel after dinner and left them to it. Reeves beckoned his scientific officers and all five men began to walk along the beach towards the headland, glancing up at the sky which was rapidly filling with grey clouds, blotting out the late afternoon sunshine.

In Jansen's workroom the curtains were drawn and I could hear the whirr of a projector. I slipped in and stood by the door. On a portable screen, Sue Murray's face was talking animatedly.

'There's a lot of anger among the tourist operators,' she was saying. 'We've invested millions of dollars in the resorts and no one's consulted us about our views. The whole debate's been hijacked by the Greenies and the loggers. The locals have been completely ignored. It's not right!'

The camera panned to White. What did the tourist industry think of the loggers?

'The loggers are OK,' Sue said doggedly. 'They don't create the problems. The backpackers do far more damage. They go about indiscriminately, disturbing sensitive areas, on the fore-dunes, for instance. Trampled vegetation loses its grip, you see, and when the wind gets up, the sand moves. You only need a wind of, say, twenty kilometres an hour and the dunes begin to blow away.'

White's face, interested, compelling. What was the solution as the tourist operators saw it?

'The island ought to be properly managed so everyone

can enjoy the beauty of it, as well as its timber. The residents are worried about their future. The Greenies want to just lock the island away for one or two generations and say to people, "You can't have it, but your children, or their children can." Surely if it's looked after it will last forever. The foresters are responsible people.' She stopped indignantly, her face flushed.

'What are your views on the Government inquiry?'

Sue snorted derisively. 'I'm pretty cynical about it, to tell you the truth. I think we all are. In the end it's going to be a political decision between the mills and the Greenies. The Government wants to get off the hook and no one's going to care about the residents!'

As Sue's face faded to a background shot of Paradise Palms against a sparkling sea and the distant mainland, White applauded.

'Beautiful editing, Hank.'

'Ya, you don't notice, do you?'

'Not at all. Perfect job. I explained we'd be cutting that last bit out. She was relieved. Said she knew she'd gone too far but she gets very angry. She's anxious for her future, as she said.'

I came forward to sit on the end of a bed. 'What did she say?' I asked.

White got up to open the curtains. The day had darkened considerably and he switched on the lights.

'She finished with a lovely full face to the camera and said, through clenched teeth, I might add, "It's all Hugh Grant's fault, him and his bloody MICO. Sometimes I'd like to kill him!"'

CHAPTER 13

The rain let go as we heeded the call to dinner—an iron triangle beaten with a length of pipe in the old country way, setting up a mighty racket which could be heard all over the resort. The dining-room overlooked the sea and was decorated in shades of blue from soft sky to aqua which, on a sunny day, reflected the turquoise water which lapped the wide, white beach. Now, however, the sea was dark and grey under a stormy sky and lightning split the night, showing clearly the agitated channel of deep water beyond. We made it to shelter just in time, shaking the water from our hair.

Sue Murray smilingly welcomed us, as serene and friendly as when I'd met her, giving no hint of the anxiety and anger which had taken hold of her during the interview. She showed us to a table and left us to study the menu. The cheerful room was filled with the hum of conversation. Most of the tables were occupied; only a couple stood vacant in their crisp blue and white cloths, sparkling with crystal and silverware.

The boy I'd noticed serving drinks at the pool came to take our order. He was now dressed more formally in dark trousers and a long-sleeved blue shirt with a white tie.

'How long will it rain, do you think, Jeff?' Jansen asked him.

He grinned broadly. 'No good for filming, is it? Don't you worry, Mr Jansen, it'll clear up by tomorrow. It often rains of a night here. Mitchell's got a very high rainfall. That's why we've got so many freshwater lakes—inland, that is. The ones on the coast are old creeks that got trapped when the dunes shifted. Are you ready to order now?'

We were. The menu catered for all tastes, even vegetarians like me. The food was delicious and beautifully arranged, although Annie seemed to have lost her appetite and picked at her meal and the others ate soberly with little chat. Sue stopped in her rounds to assure herself that we were being looked after and took in the scene in one quick, understanding glance.

'The lounge will be full tonight, and noisy,' she told us. 'We always have a talent quest on Tuesday night for the guests and we're nearly full. We've twenty-three guests at present. We can take twenty-eight, normally, but of course you're using a bungalow to work in and the one next to it is also empty. If you don't fancy the lounge, you're welcome to stay on in here if you'd like a quiet card game.'

There was a stir at the door which made her look around. A short, stocky man had entered, wearing a dark orange pullover and brown slacks. His ginger hair clung wetly to his scalp and his face looked as black as the storm outside. He stared across at Sue and she made a small gesture of welcome. His scowl lifted slightly and he took himself off to the end of the room where there was a small bar and heaved himself on to a stool, gazing morosely around the room. The girl at the bar obviously knew him and poured him a drink without his asking. He picked it up and drained it with an air of one who hardly noticed what he did and continued to watch the diners.

Sue chatted brightly for a minute longer, then crossed the room to the bar. After a brief conversation her angry visitor left and, after a hurried word with the waiter, she followed him.

Annie looked across at me. 'Sinclair Faraday,' she said. 'We met him yesterday. He didn't look very happy.'

'He looked bloody dangerous,' Jansen corrected. 'If I was filming him in the wild tonight, I'd want someone handy with a stun gun, eh, boss?'

Damien White stirred and nodded, smiling slightly, but made no comment. I was interested to see Faraday. Duke had said he was a man with a fairly short fuse. It seemed he was right.

'What's he doing here?' I asked.

'Perhaps the good Lord knows,' Paddy suggested. 'Sure, now, the man looks in a terrible temper. Perhaps the blessed green is not his favourite colour either.'

'I wonder if Sue's coming back?' I said. 'I wanted to ask her if I could borrow a vehicle.' I suddenly felt uncomfortable. 'I was going to the village, to the pub, after dinner.' I looked quickly at Annie. 'That is, if you don't want me to stay with you, love.'

White's quick mind calculated with the speed of a computer. 'To meet the Inspector? You're a friend of his, I take it, Micky?'

'Er—yes, I met him on a case a couple of years ago and we've been—ah—involved in others since. He's a good man and, yes, a friend.'

'Know a lot about crime, do you now?' Paddy's black eyes were alert, suspicious.

'Not at all,' I explained hurriedly. 'It's just—'

'Things happen to Micky,' Annie said flatly. 'He gets mixed up with things no normal person would.'

Jansen looked at her gently, sensing her thoughts. 'Sometimes a man can't help running into trouble,' he said, and I knew he wasn't talking about me. 'If something inside compels him to act in a certain way, take certain risks, like your friend Duke.'

Annie was silenced and I knew Jansen was recalling to her Fran's words at Luigi's.

'Awkward for you,' White said, and his voice was compassionate.

'Yes,' I agreed. 'If I see Reeves, spend time with him, you'll think I'm giving him information, spying on you.'

Annie put out her hand and laid it over mine. 'Oh, Micky, that's ridiculous,' she said firmly. 'No one would think that.'

'Is that general?' I looked around the table. Jansen eyed our linked hands.

'We don't know you, Douglas,' he said slowly, 'but if

Annie says you're to be trusted, then, ja, I will take her word for it.'

'I've nothing to hide,' O'Hara said shortly. 'You can talk away about me all night if you're short of more interesting conversation, and it's highly flattered I'd be to think I was occupying so much of your valuable time.'

Edgely stretched his long legs under the table and leaned back in his chair. 'I agree,' he said. 'Go and meet your Inspector friend. It might be useful to have an inside ear, as it were, on the police.'

Damien White looked his distaste. 'No, he can't do that,' he said quickly. 'If we trust him with our confidences, we can't ask Micky to spy on his police friends for us. Micky, you're one of our team and we certainly have no right to query your actions. Go and see the Inspector and I wish you an enjoyable night. I think I'll take up Miss Murray's kind offer and use the dining-room tonight.'

Paddy O'Hara winked at me. 'It's like the boss says,' he agreed. 'We don't fear your friendship with the policeman. Aren't our lives all open books and us as innocent as babes in this affair? Ask Jeff to let you have the keys to one of the cars. He'll get them for you.'

I felt duty bound to ask if anyone wanted to accompany me to the Hotel but, in spite of leaving Annie with Jansen, was relieved when they decided to stay at the resort and I was able to drive down the heavy, rain-soaked, rutted sand track to the village.

I pulled up outside the pub, headlights picking out the rain darts. A lightning flash illuminated the ornate iron-work and the deserted beer garden at the side and was followed by a heavy roll of thunder. The night had obviously settled for the best it could do in the noise and wet department.

I parked close to the front door, watching the cheerful glow of the lighted windows, misty with the inside warmth. The temperature had plunged with the rain and I was glad of my pullover. I waited for a fractional easing of the downpour and sprinted for the pub.

Inside was crowded. The lounge was alive with activity from a strange variety of folk from casual/smart men and neatly dressed women to youngsters in the hippy gear and the long hair and beards of the Greenies. There was a pleasant fug of alcohol fumes and the smoke from cigarettes blending with that from a fire which crackled in a deep fireplace at one end of the long room. Around it on chairs, stools, a sofa and just cushions on the floor sat a motley group, all wearing the MICO symbol, either green head-bands or armbands. In the public bar, which ran alongside the lounge and partly shared the same serving area, men and a handful of women propped up the counter or perched on stools. The men looked like rugged, outdoor types, and there was a sprinkling of what I assumed were local islanders around a cluster of small lacework metal tables at one end of the bar. The click of billiards punctuated the conversation in the Public where several youths and a girl were having a game, glancing disdainfully at intervals across the counter into the lounge beyond. There was an unmistakable air of 'us and them', the bar serving as the Mitchell Island Line.

I asked for Reeves and the barman, a tough-looking indi-vidual with a broken nose, thick rough grey hair and big calloused hands, looked me over suspiciously, but sent the plump blonde girl helping him to let the Inspector know he had company.

'You'd better wait in the lounge, mate,' he advised, and I complied. Duke's nice little range war was nothing I wanted to get involved in. I found a table in a corner created by the central bar, which jutted a metre or so into the room, and waited. In a few minutes David entered the lounge and came across to me.

'Micky! Glad you could make it. You didn't walk over, I hope. It's a hell of a night!'

'No, I borrowed one of the resort's four-wheel-drives. How's it going, David?'

'Oh, routinely, as always.' He smiled. 'Unfortunately, if there were any clues in the bush, this downpour will have done for them. Of course there was a search earlier by some of the police who are here to keep the peace at the blockade.' He looked up as the girl from behind the bar appeared at our table. 'What'll you have, Micky?'

We sipped our drinks. David's eyes roamed casually around the room but I knew, for all his relaxed air, he'd not be missing a thing. Voices were raised in the public bar, a not-too-steady demand for 'Drinks on me, everybody in the bar. Come on, mates, 'ave another on me!'

'Who's the high roller, I wonder?' David asked. 'That's quite a crowd to be buying drinks for.'

I took our glasses to the counter and glanced into the next room. A familiar figure was swaying by the bar, face flushed, a wad of notes in his hand. The barman came into the lounge bar and took my order with some annoyance.

'If you wait at the table, the girl'll come. No need for you to trouble to come to the bar.'

'It's no trouble,' I said airily. 'Isn't that the bloke from the ferry?'

'Johnnie Lowe, yeah. More money than sense, that one.' He filled our glasses.

'Ferrying must pay well,' I commented.

'Bloody tourists and all them Greenies. Lowe's run off his feet ferrying and running charter boats, him and his two offsiders. You one of them cops from the city?'

'Good God, no, I'm a writer. I was asked to take over the script when the girl from Mr White's film crew was killed.'

'Ah.' He thawed a little. 'You're pretty friendly with that cop.'

'The Inspector's a friend of mine. I was as surprised to see him here as anyone.'

For all his suspicion he was obviously avid for news, a barman's lifeblood.

'They reckon she was murdered,' he said, trying for a casual touch and just missing.

'Yes, apparently. That's why the detectives are here.'

'Bloody cops crawling all over the island,' he grumbled. 'Well, they won't get any joy from us. We don't know who did it and all the locals'll say the same. More'n likely them bloody Green bludgers next door.'

'But Damien White is seen to be a friend of the Green movement, not an enemy. Why would they want to kill one of his crew?'

'Don't bloody ask me, mate. Why'd they want to come and tie themselves to trees and lie in front of bloody bull-dozers? They're all bloody bonkers, if you ask me. They'd be likely to do anything to get a good headline. Trying to take my bloody business away from me! The timber men are welcome in my pub any time and that's for sure!'

I refrained from pointing out that the Greenies seemed to have expanded his business quite dramatically and he left abruptly as cries of 'Max, Max, where are ya, ya bludger?' grew louder. I took the drinks back to David.

'Johnnie Lowe, eh? You'd make a wonderful detective, Micky. It's that curiosity of yours. In like Flynn!'

I ignored the crack. 'He's in there, with a crowd of blokes around him, spending like a sailor!'

'Well, he is a sailor,' Reeves pointed out. 'The island trouble seems to be good for some locals.'

'Yes, the pub's certainly doing all right, and the boat charter business,' I agreed.

A burst of noisy laughter came from the public bar and, across the lounge, a small group looked up. One of the men frowned impatiently and said something to his companions. I glanced at David but he was watching the two men and the young woman with them.

The senior man in the group was elegantly dressed and groomed and looked as if he'd just stepped out of an exclusive gents' outfitters. Casual in slacks and a cream cashmere sweater, his whole manner suggested money and privilege. Sleek and comfortable-looking, his grey hair was ruffled by an expert hand rather than by a salt breeze on his yacht, but the effect was the same. The other man was a younger version of the same, his hair a light brown, his jacket Gucci, his expression sulky. The girl with them made it three of a kind, with a long, red turtleneck sweater, white slacks and a red and gold scarf tied like a band around her forehead. Her hair was bobbed short and glowed with a chestnut gloss.

'Interesting,' David commented. 'I know the older man —can't quite place him but I know his face. Now why?'

CHAPTER 14

The energy in the lounge shifted subtly as a number of the women looked towards the door with their peculiar inner radar and in their individual ways made small, preening gestures, touching their hair and glancing surreptitiously into the long mirrors on the wall. I turned around to see Sergeant Andrews making his way towards us in jeans and a moss green fisherman's jersey which set off his handsome dark looks to advantage. Heedless of the admiration he attracted, he pulled up a chair and joined us.

'Well, Harry?' David looked amused.

'Well, sir, Brian's next door doing a sterling job. The locals have quite taken him into their bosoms—or rather, one lady local with a very ample bosom.' David looked innocently at me as my eyebrows went up.

'My mole,' he explained kindly. 'Brian has had the good fortune to have attracted the attention of the buxom widow who runs the souvenir ship and has been invited into the holy of holies where we—er—"bloody blow-ins", I think it was—don't dare to tread.'

'You . . .!' I exclaimed. 'No wonder you didn't go to see who was buying the round. You knew you'd find out later.'

'I admired your speed,' David said, grinning. 'Harry, take a look—gently, please—at the table half way along the opposite wall. A gentleman in cream cashmere and his yuppie companions. Recognize him?'

Harry gave his order to the waitress who appeared at his elbow and turned as if watching her go to the bar. Several women immediately looked the other way, caught out.

'I can't take him anywhere,' David complained. 'What about it, Harry?'

'I know the man.' Harry turned back casually. 'Hell! Where was it?—Of course! Adam Wade! Millionaire property developer. He was involved in a Government scandal over land sales. Allegedly bribed the Minister to rezone a huge area of bushland to residential. It was never proved, though. Contributions to party funds. That's his niece, Samantha Murchison, with him, and her husband, Donald. She works for Wade, or did at the time. Called as a witness. Stunning chick—but a born snob. Bright, though. Can't think why she took up with Murchison. He's a bit of a dill, apparently—no match for her in the brains department. They say she wears the pants and tells him what to do.'

David looked pleased. 'You've got it!' he said, keeping his voice low. 'Well done, Harry.'

The waitress returned and bridled as Andrews smiled warmly at her.

'A busy night,' he said conversationally. 'I don't suppose you'll have a minute to yourself.'

'Oh, I don't know. I might manage it later —' she eyed him speculatively—'if there's a good reason.'

He winked and fished in his pocket for change. 'Here, have a drink on me. You might like to join us later for another.'

She shook her head regretfully. 'Sorry, I'd better not. The locals wouldn't like it if I was seen drinking with the Brisbane cops.' Her face brightened. 'But you might still be around when I get off at ten-thirty.'

'I might be.' Harry grinned. 'Hey, that's Adam Wade, isn't it? Don't tell me he's joined the Green movement?'

She looked highly amused at the suggestion and tossed her long blonde hair. 'That I'd like to see! No, he lives on Mitchell. Got a house up by Fisherman's Head on the north point. A real posh place. He retired here last year. Spends his time fishing and yachting. He goes down to Brissy once a month—keeping an eye on all his businesses, probably.'

'Not a very happy lot,' Harry commented.

'Better than Sunday.' She shrugged. 'They came in for a drink Sunday arvo and had a flaming row. The other bloke's married to Mr Wade's niece, and they were both having a real go at him. The girl's his niece, Samantha. Lady Muck! But she's lovely, isn't she?'

'Not my type,' Harry told her. 'Too skinny for me—and I like 'em fair. With long hair.'

'Get away with you!' She laughed, but her walk was definitely provocative as she left us. Harry turned back to his grinning chief.

'Brian rang Paradise Palms. Miss Murray said there could have been a moonlight cruise, but she's not sure. Said Lowe would know. However, White said it looked more like a vehicular ferry, or barge, but he didn't pay particular attention. Lowe reckoned he hadn't had a boat out Monday night and seemed to resent the suggestion that another operator had been taking tourists around. Seems pretty sore on that point. Wants to corner the market, I'd say. Coastguard said no one told them a boat would be out and went on about irresponsible amateur boatmen. I rang the mainland. Eversleigh's weren't using any barges—they use 'em to bring their logging vehicles back and forth, but never at night. So it remains unidentified.'

'Keep on it, Harry. Someone must have seen it other than White, if it exists at all.'

'Brian's making a few subtle inquiries of his own with Mrs Robinson. Going on about the romantic effect of moonlight on the water when I looked in to let him know where we were.'

'With the mainland so close, there'd be a lot of coming and going with private craft. Check all boat-owners on the island and mainland. If someone happened to be out there moonlight jaunting, ten to one they'd have had their binoculars trained on the resort, all lighted up. They might have seen something on the beach.'

'Right, sir.'

'It's too late now. First thing in the morning.' He turned to me. 'How is the film crew recovering?'

'They're all very quiet. They were planning a card game

in the dining-room and an early night. Sue Murray's got a
talent quest going on in the lounge. Tourist stuff, for the
guests. Tomorrow night's Hawaiian night, would you
believe? Not very Australian, but they say the visitors love
it. Apparently we're having a luau on the beach.'

'If it doesn't rain,' David commented, watching the storm
lashing the windows. 'It's a bloody night.'

'Something interesting happened though, at dinner,' I
went on, and described the Faraday incident.

'I don't blame the man for being het up,' David said. 'So
he's a friend of Miss Murray?'

'I'd say so—even more than friendship,' I agreed, thinking back. 'There was a—a closeness between them, I
thought.'

One of the MICO group around the fire began to strum
a guitar and raised his voice in a plaintive protest song in
which the others softly joined. A group of older people,
conservatively dressed, got up from their table and joined
them.

'They don't look like Greenies,' I said, surprised.

'You can't generalize any more,' David warned. 'The
Green movement isn't just a bunch of hot-headed students,
or hippies. All sorts—scientists, politicians, business people
—and all age groups are concerned with the environment.
It's a rapidly growing, world-wide movement, involving
people from every country, cutting across all the old political and social boundaries.'

I remembered the phrase, 'an idea whose time has come',
and wondered. 'I wish Annie was here. She sings a good
protest song herself.' A thought struck me and I looked at
David, puzzled.

'You told me on the ferry that Melody Scott was found
in a freshwater pool inland but had salt water in her lungs.'

He nodded, waiting.

'So that suggests she was drowned in the sea.'

'Or a salt-water pool,' Reeves nodded. 'We walked up to
the headland this afternoon. Just beyond it is the only true

rocky area on the island and it's dotted with salt-water pools.'

'Annie used to explore them when she was a kid,' I remembered. 'She came here for holidays.'

'They're filled by the high tides,' Reeves continued. 'There's no surf on the land side but I'm told the water rises quite rapidly through the channel.'

'Well,' I pursued, 'if you know she was drowned in the sea or in one of the pools, why did you ask White's people if Melody had been planning to strike inland and had perhaps changed her mind about going along the beach? Surely it's obvious that she was killed on the shore and carried inland to make it look as if she'd had an accident and drowned in the fresh water.'

Harry coughed but David just looked at me gravely, waiting for the penny to drop. When it did I flushed in sudden anger.

'You did it on purpose—to trap them!' I exploded.

'It seemed like a good idea at the time,' David said, almost apologetically. 'You see, if one of them was guilty, surely they'd have said at once that yes, Miss Scott had talked of going inland, to support the evidence of where they left the body.'

I stared at him. 'But they didn't, did they? They all swore she'd meant to walk along the beach.'

'They did.'

'Well, then, by your theory, they're all completely innocent.'

'Ah well, we've a way to go yet,' David murmured, 'but I haven't said I think any of them are guilty, you know. Just investigating every area.'

'You realize, to drown her in the salt water, then carry her up the dunes to an inland lake, must have taken a pretty strong person?' I pointed out.

'You mean, not your Annie? Miss Scott was a fairly small girl, you know.'

I glared at him and was about to argue further when

there was a burst of applause from the Greenies, who were looking towards the door. We followed their example. In the entrance to the lounge stood Hugh Grant, and beside him, Duke Jordan and Peta Ryde.

CHAPTER 15

Hugh was welcomed by his group like a conquering hero, and practically dragged to a seat by the fire by his enthusiastic supporters. Duke and Peta stopped at our table. Peta's cheeks were rosy as she looked at me and she didn't meet my eyes, but made a thorough job of wiping the rain from her colourful glasses, only looking up as I introduced her to my companions.

'What on earth are you doing here?' I asked them.

Duke grinned. 'I'm with Hugh. We came over by motor-boat to join the blockade. Well, he did. I came to suss out the situation.' He cast a warning look at me and I remembered that he'd been asked to investigate on the quiet, which was presumably not for police consumption. 'And Peta came—with me,' he finished lamely.

I eyed him. If there's one thing I know about Duke, however far away, however long away from Fran, he doesn't mess with other women.

'Where are you staying?' I asked. 'I should think the hotel's full.'

'Grant is joining the MICO camp in the forest and I'll be here and there,' he said vaguely. 'Peta needs a bed, though.'

'Sue Murray's got a spare cabin,' I remembered, 'unless it's already booked. But —' I was suddenly struck by a brilliant thought—'why don't you stay in Annie's bunga-low, Peta? She'd probably love the company. She was sharing with Melody Scott when . . .' I hesitated. 'Do you two know what's been happening?'

'Oh yes,' Duke said. 'I came up this morning. Eversleigh's buzzing with the news.'

Peta replaced her glasses and looked shyly at me.

'If you think Annie wouldn't mind and I wouldn't be in the way, I'd love to stay with you—her.'

'I'm sure that would be fine,' I told her. 'You could probably help out with some of the work.'

She looked pleased, but when I offered her a chair she elected to join Duke and Grant at the fire. David pensively watched her go.

'A pretty girl,' he commented. 'There's no doubt about you, Micky.'

'What do you mean?' I asked, stung. 'If you think I'm . . . and with Peta! She's Annie's friend. Staying in her flat while she's in England. That's all.'

David and Harry exchanged glances full of meaning, just to be annoying. They succeeded! They left soon after; David muttering something about 'routine'. The waitress looked regretfully after Harry, as did various other women. I took my drink and joined Duke, resigning myself to being branded Green.

The conservationists were mostly a likeable bunch, full of *esprit de corps* and good humour, with all the verve of enthusiasts looking for converts. One or two were of the fanatical stamp so disliked by Duke and tended to see anyone who wasn't for them as against them, but the rest seemed to treat the whole situation as a high adventure with an almost holy purpose behind it. The early crusaders must have been just such a group.

'You know, in the forest, quite near our camp, there's a huge old stump of a satinay which is at least two, probably three, thousand years old!' one earnest young girl called Sally informed me with awe. 'The last of its race. Imagine! As old as the Egyptian civilization. Supposing the island had been preserved from the beginning! What a sight to show your children!'

Hugh Grant nodded seriously. 'It's ridiculous to say logging the island is compatible with its protection,' he said. 'When you log, no matter what you do, you'll never have trees of the same magnitude and stature and you can't help but change the structure of the forest.'

A young man with a charming smile, looking like a gipsy in bright clothes and a scarf knotted around his throat, agreed.

'The only way to make sure the biological value of the place isn't degraded further is to give it a higher protected status than it has now. It's not enough that it's on the National Estate register. It needs the World Heritage listing. That's what we're fighting for,' he said unnecessarily and looked pained as they all laughed at him. 'I'm really a marine scientist,' he explained to me, 'but I've also studied forests pretty extensively.'

'I didn't know Mitchell Island was protected,' I said. Sally pulled a face. 'It's part National Park and part State Forest,' she told me, 'but it doesn't make any difference. National Park areas can be used for logging and mining— whatever the Government wants, if it feels justified.'

'Then what's the point in making it a National Park?' I asked and they all applauded.

'Exactly!' the gipsy-man said, 'and this island's so rare. For one thing, it's got the highest sand dune *in the world!* Think of that! Over seven hundred metres deep. It's called "Cook's Hill". Captain Cook put it on his map in seventeen-seventy when he sailed down the coast and it was given his name. We've got something rare in all the world. That's worth fighting for, don't you think?'

'But if the foresters are using the sustainable yield system, won't that preserve the island?' I asked.

Grant shook his head. 'It doesn't work that way, although it looks good on paper. You see, the average age of the forest is becoming younger and that means that we're getting to the point where one day no one will ever see a really big tree on the island. They should have been left for posterity, not cut down for a few lousy dollars. Think about the giant redwoods in the States and the people who pay a fortune to see the oldest living things on the planet. When people come to Mitchell, and I've taken scores of them through the forest, the thing that really holds them in— oh, awe, wonder, even reverence—is the largest, oldest, grandest trees. How many people will go and get a thrill out of a young forest? There's no feeling of antiquity. It's the ancient, magnificent giants that people come to see. They're the inspiration. Why the *hell* can't people see that?' His eyes snapped behind their heavy glasses and one of the hippy types leaned over and patted him on the shoulder.

'We'll make it, man,' he comforted. 'We shall overcome, eh!'

The guitarist began to strum the popular song of the black movement and everyone joined in the stirring words, 'We shall overcome, we shall overcome one day-ay.' It was so moving and melodious that even the voices in the public bar were stilled and several faces peered through from the other counter. Johnnie Lowe's drunken voice rose loudly, words slurring. 'There's plenty more where that came from, mate, you'll see.' It was incongruous and invasive.

As the last strains of the song died away the plump waitress appeared at my elbow.

'Time, folks, pub's closing now.' She leaned across me, her hair brushing my arm, and said softly, 'I don't suppose your good-looking mate's coming back?'

'I don't know.' She looked rueful and I added, 'But he's staying at the pub, so you're bound to see him again,' which made her brighten perceptibly.

'I've got the resort's car,' I told Peta. 'Come on, love, I'll drive you over and find you a bed.' She looked at me, hesitated, then gave me her hand and uncoiled herself gracefully from the floor. We farewelled Duke and left the hotel.

CHAPTER 16

I woke with a start, shocked out of sleep by the raucous screeching of dozens of voices. I fumbled for the watch by my bed and peered at it in the early morning light. Five o'clock. A groan came from Paddy's bed. 'Divil take the blasted birds!' he swore and pulled his pillow over his head. Jansen hadn't stirred. He'd probably accustomed himself to all sorts of wild dawn noises in his line of work.

Drawn by curiosity, I slipped on a pair of shorts and my pullover and went outside. The sun was too low to reach the west side of the island and the morning was cool but fine, with a clear, pale sky. On the edge of the settlement was a stand of trees as white as if a fall of snow had startled them and in a state of constant agitation as a flock of perhaps fifty large white birds with sulphur yellow crests ruffled and swayed and screamed at each other.

The rest of the resort was quiet as I made my way barefoot down to the beach. The sand was pristine, all traces of human habitation effectively wiped out by the heavy rain. The plastic chairs had little pools of water cupped in their seats. I turned right and, with deliberate intent, began to jog northwards in the direction Melody Scott had taken not 36 hours previously. The wide white beach with its fringe of blue water curved slowly to the left as I ran, broken only by a shallow spill of fresh water where one of the many creeks crossed the sand. A large brown and white Brahminy Kite stood silently by the water's edge, watching for fish. I held my breath and eased past the beautiful bird, which eyed me but stayed its ground. After fifteen minutes I came to a rocky area and began to tread more carefully, watching for sharp edges. The rock began to widen and flatten, running out into the sea in a series of large, rough plates, cracked with long fissures which criss-crossed the surface, breaking it into slabs. The lowest area, by the water, rose about 60 centimetres in a long rounded lip and held bits of the sea captive in several fairly large pools in which various small fishes, crabs and other sea creatures lived out their lives in their restricted homes. Marine plants thrived and gave the colonies some protection. A couple of gulls peered hopefully into one pool, waiting for any action. Now the rocky area spread vastly, taking over from the beach completely, running out of sight into the low vegetation on the distant dunes to my right. I strolled on across the dark grey basalt outcrop, thrown up by some ancient volcano, exploring the pools—some quite wide and deep. Looking back, I realized I'd rounded the point. From here the resort and the long beach were out of sight. Only the deep, dark channel remained.

A great cliff in front of me towered into the sky, doing a vague impression of a human head, brooding over the water towards the mainland. This must be Fisherman's Head Rock, although I remembered it wasn't really rock but sand, highly compressed and wonderfully coloured, red and gold, white and brown and black, in long horizontal streaks through its rough surface. I could imagine it in the rays of a setting sun. It would be breathtaking.

I continued to round the Head and discovered that on the other side the sand came down in a series of shelves to another beach, secluded and deeply curved. A jetty ran out into the water and, high above on one of the ledges, was a beautiful Spanish style house of pink stone, with terraces and arches and lush gardens. A steep, winding road connected it to the jetty. At this hour it looked deserted, standing alone in its lovely, flowered setting.

Adam Wade's retirement home, I thought, and continued to stare with interest.

The jetty was wide, probably to accommodate Wade's vehicle—or vehicles as, high above me, the house extended to a pair of large double roller doors I assumed hid the garage, partially masked by a chunky Pajero parked outside.

There was movement high above on one of the pink stone terraces and I could see the girl from the night before and the young man the waitress had said was her husband moving out into the sunshine which bathed their eyrie in its early golden light. They sat at a table and another man, presumably a servant, began to set out breakfast. They were like dolls above me and I realized with a sudden shock that if I could see them so clearly, they could certainly see me watching them if they chose to look down in my direction. Embarrassed, I turned to go—to find my way horribly barred by a giant in a black tracksuit and huge, silent sandshoes.

I gasped with shock at the size of the man. He was at least seven feet tall and perfectly proportioned. He looked the peak of physical fitness and could have easily won any body-building competition you'd care to mention. The look on his face was anything but friendly and he was standing deliberately between me and escape.

I tried for a nonchalant grin which wavered helplessly and slipped sideways off my face. He had no such trouble. He showed me a wolf's mouth full of perfect teeth, his slightly over-long eye-teeth giving an excellent impression of fangs.

'Er—g'day, mate,' I managed, with only a slight husk. His expression didn't change. The predatory smile remained fixed frighteningly to his face.

'Just taking a run on the beach,' I explained, feeling guilty for no good reason. 'Better be getting back now.'

He didn't move, just exposed more of his teeth, enjoying my discomfort. We stayed there, me beginning to wilt, to my annoyance. He looked like he was trying to hypnotize a buffalo. When he'd allowed a few more painful minutes to crawl by, he finally spoke. His voice was vast and deep and seemed to vibrate through his huge frame.

'You spying on Mr Wade's house?'

I felt the menace behind the accusation. 'No, no, of course not, I was taking a run, saw the house. It's beautiful, I stopped to look . . .' I was close to grovelling like any coward. He could have picked me up and snapped me in two whenever he liked.

'Mr Wade doesn't like people coming around.'

I was horrified to find a hint of indignation rising in me. The wimp's survival manual cautions against giving cheek to seven-foot gorillas. 'It's a public beach, mate,' I heard myself saying.

'Not here. Mr Wade owns this beach.'

'I didn't know anyone could own a piece of beach.'

'Well, you know it now, mate, so push off back to where you came from. Mr Wade doesn't want to be bothered by sightseers and spies like you. So he pays me to make sure it doesn't happen, right?'

He flexed his muscles. 'Er—right,' I agreed. This was no time for heroes.

'Well, are you going?'

'If you get out of the way.'

He advanced towards me, the wolfish smile back. 'Perhaps you want me to give you a hand, mate?'

I winced and backed up. He'd be likely to do me over for fun, just to keep his hand in. I nearly dropped with thankfulness when a cheerful voice called, 'Micky!' King Kong turned with surprising speed and faced Harry Andrews.

'Harry!' I gasped. 'Nice to see you, mate.' The two of us combined might be able to pin down at least one of those huge arms. He looked calmly up at the gigantic man.

'Detective-Sergeant Andrews, Brisbane Homicide,' he intoned, producing his identification. The other examined it closely, with reluctance. 'I've come to interview Mr Wade and Mr and Mrs Murchison. Do you work for Mr Wade?'

'I'm his bodyguard,' the deep voice growled.

'Splendid! I'll want to talk to you as well. Please conduct me to the house.'

'Mr Wade doesn't like people coming up to the house. He's retired, see? He likes to be private.'

'I'm sure he does,' Harry said crisply. 'However, he is expecting me. I phoned earlier.'

'Well, you'd better be right about that. Come on, then.' He turned to me. 'And you—keep off private property.'

'Mr Wade should put up a sign,' I shot after him.

He just grinned. 'He doesn't need one. He's got me,' he said simply and walked off. Harry gave me a wink and followed.

It must have been about forty minutes since I'd left the bungalow. I retraced my steps, still slightly nauseated by my encounter. Physical violence has always sickened me. My father despaired as his attempts to interest me in such manly pursuits as boxing, wrestling and martial arts failed miserably one by one. He thought his only son was a cissy. By his terms he was probably right. He still suffers pangs of conscience, wondering where he went wrong.

I forced my mind into more pleasant channels and thought about Annie, wondering if she was up yet and if I could coax her into an early morning swim. I hoped she'd not tired herself out last night chatting until all hours with Peta. When we'd arrived back at the resort at 10.15, the talent quest seemed to be still in full fling, with gales of laughter and bright music coming from the lounge, punctuated with much applause. We'd found Annie, Jansen, White and Edgely still in the dining-room, talking quietly. Paddy had taken himself off for a smoke. When I'd walked in with Peta, Annie had shot a startled look of accusation at me that I couldn't for the life of me fathom, then, as I explained the situation, had looked embarrassed and greeted Peta with affection, agreeing immediately to share the cabin with her. However, she was obviously still upset and I caught her watching me with an odd expression once or twice. Probably still shaky over Melody Scott. I was glad when she decided to go to bed and took Peta away to settle her in.

Jansen had given me one or two curious glances himself and walked with me to our bungalow.

'Your Peta's a very beautiful girl,' he said.

I was irritated. 'She's not my Peta!' I snapped. 'What the hell's wrong with everybody? She's Annie's friend, that's all.'

'Oh, ya, is that the way it is, eh.'

'That is absolutely the way it is!' I said vehemently.

'And does Annie know this?'

'Of course, dammit! She knows there's nothing between me and Peta.'

He gave me a sideways smile and shook his head, amused by some private thought.

'Bloody mad!' I told myself.

CHAPTER 17

As I arrived back at Paradise Palms I found Duke on the bungalow verandah having an early coffee with Jansen and Paddy.

'I've come for breakfast,' he said blithely, 'and to tell you I'm going over to Eversleigh this morning. Want to come?'

'I've got a job here, Duke. I can't just wander off and leave White.'

'Pity. You'd enjoy it,' he said cryptically. 'I was just having a chat with your boss. What time's breakfast?'

'From five-thirty to nine-thirty,' Jansen told him. 'Sue caters for early risers who are taking day trips into the interior—and the fishermen among us.'

Duke rose abruptly. 'We'll wait a bit. Come for a walk, Micky.'

I followed him back to the beach, where he turned to face me.

'What's up, mate? You look buggered!'

I gave him an account of the morning so far. He whistled. 'My stars!'

'The thing is, Melody went that way with the express intention of going around the point, which is covered with salt-water pools. Suppose she ran into that big bastard and he killed her? He wouldn't have had the least trouble in carrying her inland and arranging her to look as if she'd drowned in a freshwater lake. He's probably as dumb as he's huge. He wouldn't think about them examining the water in her lungs. I tell you, Duke, the man's a maniac. I swear he was going to do me just for being on his boss's private beach!'

'But you don't kill people for trespass,' Duke objected.

'He would. He looks like a born killer. Something out of a Boris Karloff film.'

'Well, he got to you, all right! I wonder. How come Wade owns the beach anyway? You can't own beaches in Queensland.'

'He sounded pretty sure,' I said tartly, 'and I wasn't about to contradict him.'

'I'll find out,' Duke said confidently. 'I've got a contact in the Lands Department.'

Of course he has—and everywhere else! A thought rankled and I frowned.

'You didn't bring Peta up, did you? That's not your style, Duke.'

'Ah!' He looked uncomfortable. 'Well, no, she drove up and was going to book into the Colonial Pub in Eversleigh for the night and catch the morning ferry across. I ran into her in the hotel. She didn't seem to have any plans about accommodation on Mitchell—just said she needed to be here and she'd begged time off, so I brought her across. Nice girl. Seems to think a lot of you.'

'Thanks!' I said bitterly. 'Now everybody thinks she's with me and I'm not sure Annie's very pleased—although she's distressed about Melody, so that may be it.'

'I expect it'll sort itself out,' Duke said with typical optimism. 'Be nice to her, Micky. She was scared you wouldn't want her here.'

'I don't mind,' I said, thinking of that bright face framed in rainbows, 'but I don't want her to get any ideas, that's all.'

Duke just smiled irritatingly so I changed the subject.

'What are you going over to the mainland for?'

He shrugged. 'Oh, I thought I'd do an article about the police here—get the story from their point of view. How they cope with the Greenie activities, how they feel about things—just general stuff,' he said vaguely. 'After all, the police must get sick and tired of being the baddies. They're not allowed to have opinions, just be a human shield between the warring factions.'

'I thought you were detecting for Grant?' I said drily.
'Getting sidetracked?'

'Not a lot.' His eyes were sparkling and my heart sank.
It's a sure sign he's up to something.

'Change your mind and come with me,' he offered cheerfully. Fat chance! I wouldn't be caught within a mile of the
Duke in this mood. Well, I try not to be, anyway.

We made our way through the interminable soft sand to
the main house. The constant slipping and shifting under-
foot was getting on my nerves. The thought of all those
tonnes of sand underneath me, with no safe bedrock, no
soil, depressed me.

'They had quite a time after you left last night,' Duke
was saying, 'trying to get that drunken bloke with all the
money to leave. The big spender kept telling us all how
young the night was.'

'That was Johnnie Lowe, the ferryman,' I told him. 'He
owns Lowe's Island Tours so, between ferries, he's running
tourists about. He's got a couple of blokes working for him,
apparently. He does charters, fishing trips, moonlight
jaunts, that sort of thing, and the ferry three times a day.'

Hugh Grant was at our table, head together with Damien
White. Annie, still subdued, sat next to Jansen with a
defiant look at me. My heart sank as I quickly took the
chair next to her and smiled good morning. Paddy was
explaining his job to Peta, who looked slightly nervous as
Duke and I arrived. Duke gave her a conspiratorial wink.
I could have kicked him. Jansen's eyes watched it all while
he drawled a greeting, before turning back to Annie.

'That's why Australians call a look-out a "cockatoo",'
she was explaining. 'Cockatoos post a look-out to watch
for danger and he sets up a screeching to warn the flock if
any predators—or humans—are around. He "keeps
cockatoo".'

I joined in with as much nonchalance as I could muster.
'It's a magnificent sight. You ought to film them, Jansen.'
'I have done this already.' He looked amused. 'Yesterday

morning. Sue Murray told me about their habit so I timed myself to wake before they did. As you say, Douglas, a wonderful sight. Although I do not think Craig appreciated being out of bed so early to record them.'

The tall sound engineer looked up from a generous plate of eggs and bacon. 'Needs must when Hank drives,' he said pensively. 'Part of the job.' He'd come in early and was half way through seconds. His capacity for food was spectacular, but his thin body defied me to guess where he put it.

The breakfast was serve yourself from a buffet which was well stacked with a variety of bread and fruit juice, as well as cereals, fruits, yoghurt, sausages, eggs and bacon. Sue Murray certainly fed her guests well and her staff of bright young things buzzed cheerfully about, serving individual pots of fresh brewed coffee and tea. We ate and discussed our plans for the day. There didn't seem to be anything for me, but Peta had been taken under O'Hara's wing as his assistant and his dark eyes rested appreciatively on her from time to time.

Sue stopped at our table, running her eyes over our plates, checking the service was in order.

'You probably won't want to join the luau tonight,' she said. 'Just say, and I'll make other arrangements for your dinner.'

White nodded his thanks. 'However, I think a little bright company will do us all good,' he said, 'I will certainly come for a while. We'll be attending the meeting tonight.' He looked at me. 'There's a protest meeting in Eversleigh to allow the townspeople to express their views. It should be interesting. We've hired a motorboat to go across but we can have dinner at this luau beforehand.' He eyed my empty plate. 'Micky, if you've finished, might we have a word?'

I moved back my chair. 'Right, boss.' I went out with him on to the wide verandah overlooking the now bright sea with its iridescent carnival glass waves. Over the channel the terns wove their spiralling pattern against the morning sky, making shadows to startle the fish population. The inevitable oyster-catchers bustled about on the water's edge, winkling open their breakfast with long red bills. Early strollers were sauntering along the beach, a couple were jogging.

White leaned against the verandah rail, which was natural wood, dark gold and clear varnished, as were most of the timber floors, walls and steps in the house and bungalows. Satinay, probably from the island itself and perfect for housing, being extremely hard and water-resistant. It was Queensland satinay which was used to rebuild the London docks after they were bombed in World War Two. I watched White watching the glossy, dark, restlessly moving channel and waited for him to get around to whatever was on his mind.

'Micky, I'm going to ask a very big favour of you, I'm afraid.'

'Ask away.' I grinned. After all, how bad could it be?

'Mr Jordan has been telling me some of your—er—forays into crime-solving. He seems to think you a gifted amateur detective.'

I grimaced. This sounded ominous.

'Load of rubbish,' I said briefly. 'Duke exaggerates. It just happened that once or twice, well, three times, I got involved in situations and was able to help a bit. Nothing more.'

He turned his back on the sun-bright scene and looked at me earnestly.

'Micky, this business with Melody is extremely serious and I need to know what was the reason behind her—murder.' He got the word out with obvious reluctance. 'The islanders, as Mr Jordan predicted, are a very close community and have a certain hostility towards the police. I think people probably know things they would not divulge unless forced to. Mr Jordan says it's the Australian way.'

'Mateship,' I said briefly. 'The great, if misguided, Aussie tradition.'

'Mr Jordan warned me that you would not appreciate

his interference but, as he pointed out, you are in a unique position—not with the police, neither with the conservationists. With your—er—flair for finding out the truth, you could perhaps ask questions, search around, find out if Melody's death was a deliberate attempt to stop our documentary—or something entirely unrelated.'

Bloody Duke, I thought, I'll murder the bugger! 'Look, Mr White, boss,' I floundered, 'you don't want to listen to the Duke's ravings. The police are good. They'll get to the bottom of this. I'm not the person for the job. Anyhow, what about the film script? I can't just go swanning off and leave you in the lurch . . .'

He smiled gently, a touch pleadingly. 'Paddy will take over the script. Miss Ryde will look after much of Paddy's other responsibilities. It was a good thing you invited her to join us. She'll be invaluable.'

Bloody hell! I thought. Now he's doing it!

'The thing is —' he lowered his voice—'if it was an attempt to stop the film and we continue our work, we may all be in grave danger. Anyone could be next—myself, Paddy, Annie . . .'

Like I said, a shrewd man, Damien White, he knew which button to push. I hesitated. He took advantage of my obvious dilemma and put the boot right in. First he gave a quick look around to make sure we were still alone, then he pulled an envelope out of his shirt pocket.

'It arrived this morning,' he said gravely, 'delivered, by hand, under my door. Please read it.'

The envelope was printed, addressed simply to Damien White. The message inside was also printed. It was short and to the point.

You'd better get your facts straight, Mr White. It wouldn't be very smart to believe anything Faraday says. He's got all Eversleigh in his pocket. If you say in your film that Mitchell Island should be logged you or one of your lot could be in serious trouble. There could be all sorts of accidents. If you take advice you'll listen to Hugh Grant. This is a friendly warning.

I swallowed, my throat suddenly dry. White took the letter.

'I'll be giving this to the Inspector. I haven't told the others yet. I thought I'd wait for Inspector Reeves's advice. It may not be a genuine threat, but who can tell?' Then he added thoughtfully, 'Of course, if you felt you would be able to investigate a little, you would be retained on the payroll. I don't expect you to give your time without compensation.'

'Let me get this straight,' I interrupted. 'You want to hire me as a private detective to investigate Melody Scott's murder?'

He smiled gratefully. 'Yes, that's right.'

My nerves all twanged at once. Frigging hell! I thought, David Reeves's going to love this!

I opened my mouth to decline. He'd have to like it or lump it. I'm not that stupid!

'All right, I'll do it!' I said.

CHAPTER 18

The speedboat shot across the channel, making a joke of the distance. Duke, at the wheel, glanced back at me.

'Cheer up, old son,' he said. 'You made the right decision.

'I'm not talking to you, you berk,' I growled, still seething. Duke chuckled, not a care in the world.

A couple of drifting pelicans obligingly moved over as we tied up to the jetty where the *Island Queen* was taking on board her ten o'clock passengers. Lowe, looking unbelievably cheerful after his major binge, was supervising the packing in of the cars while his young offsider gathered in the dollars. More booze money for the captain.

We took the Capri for the short drive into town and, obedient to Duke's wishes, I pulled up outside the Post Office. There was a large notice on the wall calling the residents of Eversleigh to attend the protest meeting that night in the Town Hall to make their feelings known to the Government ministers who had been invited to speak. Also on the agenda were Sinclair Faraday, Tom Eversleigh and various local interest groups. Duke read it through.

'Good one! We ought to be there. Now, let's get to work.' He disappeared into a phone-booth leaving me to chat up the postmistress, a tough job. She was fifty-plus, with short iron-grey hair, no-nonsense spectacles, a stern brown suit and sensible shoes. She answered my tentative query about any mail being left for me efficiently and dauntingly. She didn't have to be sociable with an outsider who might or might not be a Greenie and she got on with her work, leaving me wondering what to do next.

Duke breezed in and leaned over the counter, a walking charm school, his irresistible energy crackling almost visibly.

'Sorry to be a bother,' he murmured, 'but could you check and see if there's any mail for me? Richard Jordan?'

I was surprised to find there was, a registered package, which necessitated identification being produced and the book being signed, giving Duke ample time to use his famous conning techniques, although he winces when I use the term. By the time he'd got the package, clearly marked 'Richard Jordan, Journalist' in his hands, the postmistress was fully aware that this was *the* Richard Jordan, that he was here to do a story on the effect of the Mitchell Island Green blockade on the local townsfolk and her opinion would be not only welcome but the story would probably be second rate without it.

She blushed and simpered, I swear it, and said, 'Oh, Mr Jordan, well, in that case . . .' and then talked nineteen to the dozen about all the extra work it entailed and all these strangers—heaven knew *who* they were and some dressed in *most* peculiar clothes, coming in to pick up mail and wandering around Eversleigh setting a bad example to the local children—'Young people are so susceptible to all sorts of odd influences'—and did he hear about the bomb in Brisbane? What if it had been sent in the mail or someone else tried a similar thing? It made her job *dangerous*.

By now we were behind the counter, drinking tea with her, me having been introduced as Duke's 'associate'. Duke exuded sympathy and understanding, storing it all away in his computer brain, his quick Gemini mind always one step ahead.

'I suppose all the people on Mitchell have the mail held here. You must get to talk to them all. I expect you have a very balanced view of the situation—I can see they'd talk to you.' That's laying it on a bit thick, I thought, but Duke hadn't overdone it. She explained that the resort's mail was taken over on the midday ferry, as well as that of most of the permanent residents. People like Adam Wade, such a nice man, picked his up from the Post Office or sent that huge assistant of his in. Sinclair Faraday collected his own.

His piled up, of course, as he wasn't always on the island, but he managed to come in at least twice a week, or that lovely Sue Murray might pick it up for him if she was in Eversleigh.

Duke expressed sympathy with the forester's point of view. It was a problem, wasn't it? Did she worry about the future of Eversleigh?

'Oh, I do, of course, although there would always need to be a Post Office here to serve the town and farms and the island. But it's a very difficult time for us. Mr Faraday was looking quite ill under the strain of it all when he was last in for his mail. He's usually pleasant and friendly—we have our little joke about how we'll have to build another room here for his mail now he gets so many protest letters and that sort of thing, but this time he was quite abrupt and looked very angry.'

'When was this, do you remember?'

'Well, I do. It was late on Friday, four o'clock. He was all right at first, looked quickly through his letters for anything important, as he always does, and one letter caught his eye. He ripped it open and read it—it was quite short—then swore as if he'd forgotten I was there. His face was quite thunderous. He stormed out without a word, so you can see how upsetting it is for him. He has the full support of the local people, and he knows it, but for all that, the strain is certainly telling.'

Duke's eyes were alight. We chatted some more, finished our tea and said our farewells.

'I'll drop in again for a chat, and my mail,' Duke said, 'but I expect you're so busy you'd rather I didn't.'

She bridled. 'Any time at all, Mr Jordan. Such a pleasure. You gentlemen are always welcome.'

'Smooth bastard,' I told him as we drove away. 'Who's the package from?'

'Me,' he said smugly. 'I thought I might need an excuse to chat. Postmistresses always know all the gossip, so I mailed it to myself before I left.'

I accorded him a respectful silence before asking, 'Where to now?'

'Police Station,' he said briefly. 'I want to find out about these two hot-headed Greenies.'

'I thought you were convinced they dunnit,' I told him.

'I was, until it occurred to me, how did they know that Brent Eversleigh would be crossing the road just at that time to catch the train? They can't have been wandering the streets in their little Rover trusting to chance to deliver him under their wheels. I read the reports again. The vehicle was stationary, up the road, just minutes before he crossed. As soon as he hove into view, it went for him. Couldn't miss—but it couldn't get up to top speed in the space available, so that, no doubt, is why he's still alive and improving slowly. Now, either it was a whopping great coincidence that they just happened to be up the street, saw their hated enemy, and went for him bald-headed on the spur of the moment, or it was premeditated, which means someone close to him with the right info.'

'Who knew his plans?'

'Myself, Hugh—and I assure you we had nothing to do with it—Melody Scott, who had the schedule of interviews, Damien White, although I doubt if he remembered who he was seeing when, Brent's father Tom Eversleigh and probably others of his family. He'd know who he told but he's still in intensive care and not even the police can get in to talk to him.'

'Try smarming your way in,' I suggested.

'Bastard!' he said, without heat.

Duke's performance at the Police Station would have won him an A.F.I. award for best actor. It was run on similar lines to his victorious capture of the Post Office. The uniformed sergeant, an overweight, morose man in his late forties, gave us police coffee which we drank to be polite, and unburdened his soul to the big city journo. A good, sympathetic story would put him firmly back in the notice of his superiors who, he suspected, had forgotten his existence—and put him in line for promotion.

'It's not easy,' he complained, 'and now the bloody detectives from Brissy have taken over and I'm not getting a look-in. No chance to show what I can do. I told them I could handle it, with young Graham. Trouble was, the detective-sergeant's tied up out of town on one of the farms. One of the hands gone missing after a brawl—looks very sussy—so I had to call in Brisbane Homicide, and from there on, did they listen to me?'

'You'd have a good chance of finding out about the attempt on Eversleigh, though,' Duke soothed, 'with Deakin and Hall in gaol. I assume they're still here?'

'Oh yes, just as if we've got a hotel out the back and bugger-all to do except run around after them,' he said sourly, 'waiting for the smart Brisbane cops to interview them. I'm feeding them, looking after them like a bloody nursemaid, meals from the pub three times a day, all at the Station's expense. Politics!' He snorted. 'If I'd my way I'd get up 'em so fast they'd tell me the truth all right, but I'm not allowed to question them because of bloody politics!' His disgust was written all over his heavy face. Then he brightened suddenly.

'Anyway, we've found their bloody vehicle. Hidden off a track outside town, and covered with branches. Local farmer found it this morning when some of his cattle strayed. We'll soon get 'em to admit they done young Brent.'

Duke digested this, then smiled cheerfully at the disgruntled sergeant.

'Any chance of us talking to them?'

'Not on your bloody life, mate, unless you can get the Commissioner to OK it. I wouldn't risk it otherwise.'

'I'll see what I can do,' Duke said blithely. 'He owes me one.'

'Christ!' The sergeant stared at him. 'Put in a good word for me, mate.'

'Will do. C'mon, Micky, we'd better get on. Thanks, Sergeant. We'll probably be back. OK?'

'Fine by me, mate. Ask your friend the Commissioner.'

We left him to his bitter reflections.

'Does the Police Commissioner really owe you a favour?' I asked curiously.

'Actually, he does. I kept quiet about one or two things after the previous Commissioner was sacked and the new man came in. After all, he deserved a fair go to clean up the force, so I laid off. He said he was grateful. Now we'll see, eh! Let's have lunch.'

We stopped once again at the Post Office for Duke to use the phone, then drove back to the waterfront to the Colonial Hotel, a typical two-storey Queensland pub, like its mate over the channel on Mitchell. Verandahs, lace ironwork, corrugated iron roof, beer garden with white metal tables where groups were gathered in the shade. In the foyer one wall was hung with old photographs from the early days of Eversleigh and the faces of its early citizens, men with drooping handlebar moustaches, women in bonnets and shawls, looked down on the present-day customers. A huge colonial sideboard stood against a wall with a collection of old crockery, tureens, plates, dishes, in a Dutch blue pattern.

We found the dining-room which followed the Colonial theme for the tourists. Tableaux were posed around the walls, roped off from the public. Shop dummies dressed in pioneer costumes sat at spinning wheels, stood arm in arm in front of an old-fashioned camera for their portrait, rode an old penny-farthing. One, in the guise of a bushranger, held up a mural of a coach, with the painted passengers' startled faces peering out. It was well done and gave the room the feeling that it had time-travelled back a hundred years. One of the models had a fashionable short wig, which was the only incongruous note. All but one of the men wore long beards and moustaches like the photographs in the foyer.

We were the only diners. The waitress got the Jordan treatment as we checked the menu. Colonial names for the food, of course, and you could have billy tea and damper with golden syrup. We ordered and I flicked out my napkin in preparation. The linen was green to match the walls, and arrangements of dried native flowers were on each table, giving a sense of the bush. I ignored Duke's snap judgement of 'kitsch!' as he glanced around. I happen to like the odd lashing of kitsch. I'm a tourist at heart.

The waitress returned to summon Duke to the phone. 'I told them I'd be at the pub for lunch,' he explained. 'Won't be long.'

'I'll wait until he's back,' I told the girl. She had a bright smile and an obvious willingness to chat to anyone who offered. I grinned at her. 'I thought you'd be flat out like everyone else with the extra people in town.'

'They're all in the beer garden,' she said. 'There's a local folk group sings Colonial songs out there. Don't get too many of the Greenies spending their money in the dining-room. And a good thing, too,' she continued with a sniff. 'Vandals, they are, if you ask me.'

I raised a questioning brow. It was all the encouragement she needed to blacken the Greens.

'I had some in the other day,' she explained, 'and they damaged the place. You wouldn't believe. Vandalized the displays and cut up the napkins. Getting at the hotel because the islanders use it and Mr Faraday stays here, I bet. If they set foot in here again, I'll turn them out, quick smart. We can do without their sort making trouble.'

Duke joined us and the indignant girl went to order our lunch.

'Great!' he enthused, when she was out of earshot. 'I've got the dope on Wade's beach. You're right, Micky, the smart bugger bought it a few years back. Let me tell you how.'

CHAPTER 19

I stared expectantly at Duke.

'Do you remember that big scandal just before the last Government lost the election? It was a couple of months after Hugh won his court case over Mitchell. The Japanese developer who was planning to build a huge resort up north and wanted to buy the beach front?'

I nodded. It caused riots at the time from angry North Queenslanders objecting strongly to the idea of being barred from their own beach. Something struck a chord in my memory. 'Who was that bloke?' I asked, although I thought I knew. 'The Japanese?'

Duke grinned. 'Just coincidentally,' he said, 'Dan Nishida. If you recall, the Government pushed through a bill in one of their infamous all-night sittings, changing the legislation to enable the sale to go ahead. They were, of course, heavily—er—compensated in the usual way. Large contribution to Party funds. Well, in the end the resort didn't get built because they'd signed an agreement to be at a certain stage of development in six months from the signing of the contract and they weren't even started; so public opinion forced the Government to cancel the deal.'

I remembered all too clearly. It was in the papers and TV news for months while the Government tried every way to hold on. In the end they had to give in, one of the rare times the people actually won.

'The law was repealed as soon as the new Government took over,' Duke continued, 'but during the short time it was in place Adam Wade, very quietly and after a suitably large sum found its way into the Party coffers, slipped his sale through. So, even though the law was changed, he owns his piece of beach, all legitimately. It can't be overturned.'

'Then why does he keep it such a dark secret,' I asked, 'if it's all fair and above board?'

'Ah! We'll have to find out.'

A group of business men came in and selected a table. The waitress promptly appeared with menus. I glanced idly around and got the shock of my life to see Godzilla in the doorway.

'Bloody hell!' I whimpered, turning a shocked face to Duke. 'That's the maniac who nearly killed me this morning!'

Duke looked up with interest. 'Grief! He'll be a big lad when he stops growing.'

'Ha, bloody ha!' My voice was notches too high. 'What the hell's he here for?'

The muscled giant looked slowly around, his eyes pausing a while as he sighted me. He showed his teeth, then stepped back through the door. I was clammy with relief.

Almost immediately Adam Wade entered, followed by the Murchisons. They went to a table at the far end of the room by a window which gave a sweeping view of the beach and jetty. In the distance, the ferry was half way across the channel, returning from the midday run.

A second woman appeared and went immediately to their table. She had the look of a manageress, smartly dressed and groomed. Personal service from the top for the Wade clan. Our waitress returned and set out our meal.

'That's Adam Wade, the millionaire,' she whispered, 'and his niece and her husband. They came up on Friday night and stayed here and Mr Wade met them for breakfast before they went over to the island on Saturday. They always have that table. It's got the best view, and Mr Faraday has the one next to it.'

'I suppose you get a lot of regulars who want their own rooms and tables.' Duke smiled at her.

'Oh yes, people working on the island, waiting for the morning ferry. If they've been down to Brissy, for instance, they come up late sometimes, like Mr Faraday. He has his regular room. We never know when he'll be staying. He uses the ferry.'

'When was he here last?' Duke asked casually, showing just enough interest.

'Let me think—oh, yes, it was Friday. He came up too late for the ferry and stayed the night.'

'Now he'd be a man with a lot on his mind.' Duke sounded sympathetic. 'It can't be very pleasant to be in his position.'

'No, I feel sorry for him,' she agreed. 'He was all washed out on Friday night. Looked like death. And at breakfast. Then at lunch on Saturday he was so quiet you couldn't get a word out of him, poor bloke.'

She bustled away. Duke ate thoughtfully. 'Whatever was in that letter seems to have knocked Faraday for six,' he commented finally. 'I wonder what the hell it was! I don't suppose he'd tell me.'

'Sue Murray might know,' I said, and told Duke of the incident at dinner the previous night. 'She's certainly his confidante.'

'Have a shot at finding out, then,' Duke said. 'You're at the resort.'

'Honestly, Duke, I'd rather not,' I objected. 'I hate all that stuff. It's none of my business and I never know what to say.'

'It'll be your business fast enough if anything happens to Annie,' he said tartly.

After lunch we went back out to the Capri, me looking about nervously in case my *bête noire* was still hanging about. I couldn't miss him, he was sitting with folded arms on a chair outside the dining-room. He seemed to bear me no ill will but when he showed his wolf's smile, I shuddered.

Safely in the car, I asked, 'Now what?'

'Back to the Police Station, I fancy,' Duke said. 'If my phone call worked, the sergeant should let us in to see the prisoners. Oh, first I want to go past the Railway Station.'

The Station was in the centre of town on the main street

named, appropriately, Arthur Street. Opposite was a row of shops and offices, and all had pasted up notices about the protest meeting. No one could fail to know it was on. Duke pointed out the office of Eversleigh and Sons Pty Ltd.

'Brent Eversleigh left from there to catch the train,' he explained. 'He arrived early at the office to do some work and left just before ten for the Brisbane Express. He popped into the newsagent's next door for the paper at six-thirty. Apparently he often came early to work to get a few hours in before the staff arrived at nine, although, being Saturday, there wouldn't have been anyone else there. Pull over, Micky. Let's scout around.'

I drew up obligingly and found a space outside the station. Crossing the road, I thought how good it was to be on the mainland with safe, solid ground under my feet.

'The mill used to be here,' Duke told me, 'but they shifted it out of town in the 'fifties and just keep their head office in Eversleigh now.'

We entered the newsagent's which was directly opposite the station. Duke bought a paper, did his thing. The man serving adopted us as long-standing cronies immediately and became loquacious, thumping the counter with a stubby fist, his round face florid.

'I can give you a story, you just listen,' he shouted. He was short, rotund and red-faced and looked like a candidate for a heart attack. 'I seen the whole bloody thing, mate. Seen young Brent cross the road, seen him hit. Hell's bells! It was a shocker! Bloody bang like a bomb going off and he flies up into the air and drops like a bloody stone. Them Green bastards should be strung up and if we had our way they bloody would be.'

'So you saw the people in the vehicle?'

'Gawd, no, couldn't see that clearly in here. Just seen Brent being bloody totalled. Vehicle took off like a bat outa hell. They hid it, you know, but the cops have got it now. Artie McKenzie practically run right into it chasin' his bloody stock. Anyway, after they left it in the bush, the bastards front up to the cop shop with a phoney story.'

'You think it was just a story?'

'What else? I may not have seen them, mate, but Johnnie Lowe did.'

Duke put on his sympathetic tell-me-all-about-it face which never fails to get results.

'Look, it was like this. Saturday morning, see! Pretty busy outside, people shopping and that. Supermarket next door. Johnnie's in here, standing right where you're standing, Rick. Came in for cigarettes and the *Sun*. Then we hear the roar of an engine, really revving, and we look up. Rover comes flying along and I seen Brent in the street. "Shit, they'll hit him," I yell, and Johnnie hares out on to the footpath. See where that sheila with the pram is? Right there, he was. Crowd of people on the footpath, all stopped to see what's going on. Poor Brent cops it, tyres screeching, and the Rover sort of rocks about and tears off. Everyone's screaming and carrying on, running out to help Brent, and there's blood everywhere. Johnnie comes back in, white as a sheet, and bloody pukes all over the floor. Then I call the ambulance but Doc Jenner whose surgery is next to the chemist up there, he comes out and brings his bag and starts to get everybody away from Brent. That's just how it was, Rick, just like I said.'

Duke looked impressed. 'You'd make an excellent witness,' he said admiringly. 'That's very graphic.'

He shook his head slowly, face darkly flushed. 'I'll never forget it as long as I live. Cold-blooded murder, or would have been—and will be if young Brent doesn't pull through. I'm glad I couldn't see very much, Rick, that's for sure!'

'And you say there was a crowd on the pavement?'

'Too bloody right! Three or four deep, from the edge of the road to my shop. Bloody lucky Johnnie seen 'em, because nobody was sure of anything, all giving conflicting reports to the cops.'

'I suppose he told the police right away and gave a description?'

The newsagent mopped his face. The afternoon was warm and he wasn't built for the heat.

'He was too busy puking on my floor,' he said scornfully. 'Right where you're standing, Rick. Wouldn't have known what he seen. But he remembered later, and went around to Col Ryan at the cop shop and give his statement. Come in here first. "Jack, I've remembered," he says. "I seen them two Green bastards, clear as anything, and I'm going around to see Col about it." And off he went.'

'Right, excellent,' Duke said absently.

We left and walked slowly along the footpath, past the supermarket, chemist and doctor's surgery. Duke was silent, his brain wrestling with some private thought. Then he stopped abruptly as a man crossed our path and entered the next building. Duke let his breath out in a little hiss and stared at the name on the façade: Austral Development Real Estate Office. He looked at me, back in the now, excitement blazing in his speaking eyes.

'Recognize that man?' he demanded, keeping his voice low.

'Should I?'

'Only if you paid any attention to Hugh's court case against the Government. That was Bernie Wilson.'

'Of the Wilson/Nishida Group?'

'The very same! Now, what's Wilson doing up here again and in the local Real Estate Agency?'

He turned suddenly and began to sprint back to the car. Once more I chauffeured him to the Post Office where he enriched the coffers of Telecom for quite some time.

CHAPTER 20

I yawned, bored, waiting for the Duke to finish his phone calls, and let my attention rove to a pretty little memorial park over the road from the Post Office. A typical feature of Aussie country towns, in the middle of the immaculately mowed lawn a bronze soldier stood on his stone plinth on which was inscribed the names of Eversleigh's sons who had heeded their country's call and fought and died in two world wars. On Anzac Day the plinth would be buried deep in floral tributes and as daylight glimmered into the sky, the Last Post would echo in the cool autumn morning for the dawn service; and all Eversleigh would be here, silently remembering those who would not grow old as we who are left grow old and who refused to be forgotten.

Sparrows hopped about the bright garden beds and laid siege to a solitary figure sitting on a white wooden bench. My wandering eye stopped, riveted to his back. It looked a lot like Adam Wade sitting in the quiet park, reading a paper. After a couple of minutes he stood up, looked at his watch and, ignoring the litter-bin, tossed the folded paper on to the seat. Millionaires don't have to live by the rules of the herd, I thought, annoyed. Suddenly another familiar figure appeared and stood looking after the rich litter-bug. After a moment he shrugged and picked up the paper, glanced at the headlines, then tucked it under his arm and went off whistling. I grinned to myself. Wade probably read the *Financial Review*, so there wouldn't be a lot in it to interest Johnnie Lowe—unless the ferry captain thought he could double his money by reading it. Then Duke was settling himself on the passenger seat, and we slid away from the kerb. I turned in the direction of the police station, a block away.

'What did you find out?'

'Well, after a few false starts, I got on to my Deep Throat at the *Courier-Mail* and he did some fast digging for me and called me back straight away. It seems Austral Development is actually the parent company of Wilson Properties and Bernie Wilson is on its board of directors. Which is why they did the Nishida deal through him rather than showing their hand openly. A lot of the locals didn't like it and the islanders kicked up a hell of a stink.'

'Then Wilson's being here is probably quite innocent,' I mused.

'Nothing that shark does is innocent,' Duke said shortly. 'I wouldn't trust him to the end of the street!'

Col Ryan's brow raised as we walked into the police station.

'I don't know how you wangled it, mate, but the big brass have been on the blower. You're to have access to the prisoners and my full cooperation. But there'll have to be a constable with you the whole time. That's the deal, take it or leave it!'

'We'll take it.' Duke grinned. 'Thanks, Sergeant.'

'It's not my bloody idea,' he said morosely. 'At least the smart-arsed Brisbane detectives have let me have my constable back. He'll show you in.'

We were left in a small box of an interview room. Minutes later, two young people were ushered in. They looked frightened and eyed us warily as they were motioned to two chairs on one side of the only table. Duke and I took the other two which were set opposite and Constable Graham stood woodenly by the door and gazed over our heads.

I looked the pair over as we introduced ourselves, feeling a good deal of sympathy for their plight.

'Do you know who I am?' Duke asked them. The boy, Jeremy Hall, nodded, his anxious eyes fixed hopefully on Duke's face.

'I'm trying to get to the bottom of all this,' Duke told them, 'and I'll tell you right now I think it's most unlikely you were involved. However, I need you to go over your story again in as much detail as you can.'

Barbara Deakin dropped her head in her hands and her long hair fell forward, hiding her face. 'Oh Christ,' she sobbed, 'everyone here thinks it was us. We can't get anyone to believe us.'

Hall put his arm around her. 'It's OK, Babs, don't cry, darling.' He looked at Duke. 'We've had a hell of a time.'

Duke frowned. 'Ill-treated?'

Hall glanced at the constable nervously. 'N—no, just the opposite, but no one believes us, as Babs says, and they won't let any of the MICO people see us.'

'Do you have a solicitor?'

'Yes, but of course he's local, so I think he's simply doing the minimum possible required by the law.'

'I'll organize someone from Brisbane for you who won't be biased. Hugh will see to it.'

'Thanks.' The young man with the heavy brown beard had a natural dignity. 'Do stop, Babs. We're getting help at last.'

'All right, now tell us what you remember.'

'We remember every little detail. We've been over it again and again. God, it's a nightmare!' He paused, sorting his thoughts. 'We came up from New South Wales—Lismore—to join the Green blockade. I'm with the University there studying agriculture and Babs is a student teacher. We both belong to MICO and Hugh put out a call for help.'

Barbara Deakin lifted her tear-stained face and shook back her light brown hair. Her eyes were hazel but the red rims didn't suit her. She took Hall's handkerchief and wiped her face, ending with a firm blow of her pert nose, and said shakily, 'We got here in heaps of time for the morning ferry. We left Lismore on Friday afternoon and slept in the back of the Land-Rover in a rest area. We were here at eight-thirty, got our permit from the Parks and

Wildlife Office and went down to the jetty to wait for the boat.'

'At about eight forty-five.' Hall nodded. 'We didn't feel like hanging around and there was nobody else in sight and no sign of the ferry and we hadn't had breakfast, although we'd bought some fruit and sandwiches at a roadhouse a few miles out of Eversleigh . . .' He paused for breath.

'So we left the Rover on the jetty to be sure to be first in line in case there were a lot of other vehicles crossing, and went for a walk along the beach,' Barbara continued.

'Did you see anyone?' Duke asked quickly.

'Only a couple of fishermen further up the beach, but they didn't see us—or if they did, they were too far away to identify us.'

'Still, it would prove someone was there,' Duke said. 'I'll check it out. Go on.'

'We stopped and had breakfast on the beach and paddled, just filling in time, you know,' Hall continued the story. 'We tried to get a couple of pelicans to come in close but they steered clear. We were just having a peaceful morning, looking forward to seeing Hugh and our other MICO friends and doing some good in this pathetic world.' His voice broke. 'Oh God, I'm sorry!'

The two unhappy youngsters clung to each other in desperation. Barbara bit her lip.

'I'd love a cigarette,' she said huskily. 'I gave them up when I found out how many tonnes of trees are burned each year just to cure tobacco. I thought, if I'm Green, I shouldn't smoke.' Her eyes filled with tears again. 'But I'd love one right now.'

Duke turned briskly to the constable. 'Can you rustle up a packet of cigarettes, mate?'

He stood his ground. 'Sergeant said I'm not to leave you alone with the prisoners.'

'For Christ's sake, then. I'll come with you!' Duke fumed. 'The Commissioner's going to hear a thing or two, Constable. Now, take me to Sergeant Ryan, pronto!'

Constable Graham was clearly torn between his loyalty to his sergeant and the desire to avoid any black marks with the Commissioner and began to look mulish, but Duke simply opened the door and shoved him through.

'Come on, Constable, the sooner we go the sooner we'll be back.'

As they left the room, Barbara grabbed my hand frantically.

'It's the sergeant,' she whispered urgently. 'He's a real pig. He threatens us all the time. Keeps on and on about what he'll do if he gets the chance.'

'He's taking it out on us,' Jeremy agreed. 'He lets our food go cold, pretends to forget the sugar for our coffee, that sort of thing. And he never stops the verbal abuse and snide remarks. He gets to us every way he can.'

'You should complain to your solicitor.' I felt anger rising in me at the situation of these two probable innocents at the mercy of a vindictive bully.

Barbara's grip on my hand tightened. 'We did, but nothing changed. It got worse if anything, so we're scared to say any more. He threatened to beat Jeremy up so no one would know—no bruises or anything. Oh God, Mr Douglas, I'm so frightened. Please get us out of this.'

The door opened and she quickly drew back. Duke came in cheerfully waving a packet of cigarettes which he handed to the girl. The constable was hard on his heels, looking definitely put out. Probably guessed there was trouble in store for him as soon as we'd gone.

'There you are.' Duke leaned over to light the cigarette between Barbara's shaking fingers. 'You'd better keep the lighter too,' he suggested, grinning. 'No harm done, eh, Constable?'

'Thanks, mate.' Jeremy gave him a grateful look.

The rest of their story was as we'd heard it. Arriving back at the jetty and discovering their vehicle missing, the pair had made a fruitless search of the town, then finally gone to the police station to report the loss and, to their

shock, had been arrested for attempted murder and ques-
tioned at length about the accident which they'd heard
being discussed all over town as they looked for the Rover.
No one had shown any desire to listen to, or believe their
story, constantly demanding to know where they'd hidden
their vehicle. They'd been held without bail and prevented
from having any contact with their friends, then they were
put in a line-up and later told they'd been positively identified as the guilty couple.

'Hugh tried to see you,' Duke told them, 'but he was
turned away. He would have got you legal help but was
told you had your own solicitor.'

He switched the subject in his abrupt way.

'Your Land-Rover's been found, did you know? Hidden
under branches in the bush outside town.'

Jeremy nodded. 'They told us,' he said in a low voice.
'The sergeant said they'd have us now; but —' he looked
at Duke worriedly—'why on earth would they think we hid
it like that? It doesn't make sense, does it?'

Duke shot an excited look at me, his eyes glowing. I was
damned if I could see why.

It worried me to leave them there in their helpless state
but at least we could set the wheels of justice in motion.
The sergeant looked closely at us as we left and it took all
my strength to smile at him and thank him. I was going to
take unequalled pleasure in letting Duke know how he was
intimidating his prisoners and thus putting a major spoke
in his ideas of promotion, if I knew my friend!

CHAPTER 21

I lost no time in telling my story to Duke. He sat in the Capri gazing ahead of him, his brow furrowed, fingers drumming a little tattoo on the passenger seat.

'Don't worry, mate,' he said at last. 'We'll fix him, I promise. Poor kids! We've got to find out what happened and get them out of there.'

We found ourselves once more in the main street of Eversleigh.

'Stop a minute,' Duke demanded, and I drew up a little past the scene of the accident. 'Now look! Where would you have said Lowe was standing?'

I considered. 'Well, the girl with the pram was just outside the newsagent's—by the window.'

'Not on the kerb?'

'You saw her, Duke, she was right outside the window.'

'Right! What time's the afternoon ferry?'

I glanced at my watch. 'Half an hour ago. It's two-thirty.'

'Hmmm! I want a word with Lowe.'

'He'd be back by now. It takes him roughly fifteen minutes a crossing—depending how long it takes to load the vehicles.'

We drove back to the jetty and left the Capri once more in the car park. The *Island Queen* was tied up but Lowe was nowhere in sight. Suddenly a voice hailed us and we turned to see the pretty, plump girl from the Mitchell Hotel smiling at us.

'G'day, fellas. You've missed the ferry.'

I grinned back. 'Yes, we know. We were looking for the captain.'

'Johnnie? How come?'

'For a story I'm doing about the local people,' Duke told her.

'Of course, you're that famous journalist, aren't you? Johnnie's taken a charter out for the afternoon. He'll be in the pub tonight, though. Anything I can tell you?'

'I heard he saw Brent Eversleigh's accident. I'd be interested to get his story.'

'I was in town Saturday morning,' she said hopefully.

'Did you see what happened?'

'No.' She sounded regretful. 'Would you believe it! I missed it by ten minutes!' She flicked her blonde hair back with a quick toss of her head. 'I was in the supermarket just before. Came over early because the dress shop was having a sale and I wanted to be first in. That's down the road from the Mill office. There was a beaut dress in the window I had my eye on. I got it, too,' she said triumphantly. 'Thirty per cent off. Jeeze, I was chuffed!'

Duke laughed. 'What time was that?'

'Eight-thirty. I was there at eight, though, to make sure.'

'Many people around?'

'No, just the shop people arriving for work. And I saw Mr Wade. He'd come over to pick up the Murchisons. He drove past at about eight-fifteen.'

'A bit out of his way, surely. The pub's on the waterfront.'

'Yeah, but he was seeing poor Brent. Went into the Mill office.'

'Oh?' Duke's eyes lit up. 'When did he leave, did you notice?'

She looked slightly puzzled. 'Oh, just before the shop opened. But there's nothing wrong with that, is there? They're good mates. They often get together.'

Duke shifted ground rapidly. 'Did Johnnie Lowe tell you about seeing the accident?'

'Too right!' She sounded excited. 'It was real lucky he saw what happened, although lots of people got a sort of impression what the two looked like. It made him late for the ferry. He didn't get away till ten-fifteen and copped a bit of a flak from the people waiting on Mitchell, 'cause it made them all late.' She broke off as an engine's roar sounded. Further down the beach was an inlet where an elegant white motor-launch was moored by a sturdy-looking shed. As we watched it began to nose away from its jetty and back gently around until, with a throaty burst of speed, it raised its nose out of the water and powered out towards the island.

'That's Mr Wade's launch,' the girl said. 'It's a beauty. That's his own private jetty and lock-up garage.' She reluctantly brought her envious gaze back to us.

'Have you been for a ride in it?' Duke asked.

'Don't I just wish! But Johnnie has. He does work for Mr Wade from time to time. Special charters for his rich mates, and odd jobs. Mr Murchison had him out on Saturday night, fishing, Johnnie said. Paid him real good, too. Well, if I can't tell you anything else I'd better push off. Max'll be wanting the pub's runabout back. See you fellas tonight, maybe.'

'For sure,' Duke grinned. 'And thanks!'

She looked cheekily over her shoulder. 'For what? My pleasure, I'm sure.'

We made our way past the minuscule ferry ticket office where a large painted sign advertised the ferry times. 10.0 a.m., midday and 2.0 p.m. daily. The only exception was a special late ferry on Fridays at 6.0 p.m. for people coming up to Mitchell for the weekend. Charter services were listed, specials by request, and phone numbers, presumably Lowe and his staff.

Duke looked thoughtfully at me. 'How tall would you say Lowe is?' he asked. I've got used to him suddenly asking totally irrelevant questions, and answered without comment.

'Don't know—not very tall. Perhaps five six, or five seven.'

'That's what I'd reckon,' he said briskly. 'Micky, I think we should tell Reeves about those kids at the police station and get a search started for the fishermen they saw on the beach. Also, for anyone who saw them in town looking for their Land-Rover. There must have been someone.'

I grimaced. 'He's not going to like my being involved.'

'It's not against the law to talk to people. Blame me! You can tell him you were merely a reluctant observer. Let's get back to Mitchell. We've a deal of digging to do.'

Ten minutes later we were walking down Mitchell's sandy road through the village. The souvenir shop also organized hire vehicles and Duke made arrangements with the buxom proprietress while I browsed among the tourist offerings. A group of simple charcoal sketches of the Mitchell Hotel, the jetty and various flora and fauna caught my eye. One of the locals with a bent for art. They were executed with a softness and feeling for the bush that I found irresistible and oddly familiar—and they were reasonably priced. I chose a scene of palms and took it to the counter.

'Look, Duke, it's delightful.'

Mrs Robinson glanced at it. 'That's Old Maggie's. She lives local, up above Fisherman's Head. I buy her pictures to help her out, poor soul. The tourists like them.' She wrapped my sketch in tissue paper. 'I sell a lot of locals' work. The pottery over there and the pippy shell ornaments —and the coloured sands, of course.' There was an array of different shaped bottles from tiny phials to quite large jars, all containing layers of sand in every glowing colour, some cleverly arranged in little scenes.

Mrs Robinson gave us a conspiratorial look. 'It's illegal to take the sand now, so I'll tell you a secret. This is really just ordinary sand dyed to look like the coloured sands. Looks just the same. Of course, I don't tell the tourists. What they don't know won't hurt 'em, and we make no claims that it's the real thing.'

We asked for David or his men at the Hotel but they were nowhere to be found.

'What next?' I asked, thinking of Annie and how long I'd been away.

'I want to see Hugh. He's at the MICO camp, about two

hours' drive from here. Come with me. We can talk.'

Our vehicle bounced and slid along the soft sand track climbing into the dunes. The downpour of the previous night had smoothed out the pathway, washing the sand back on to the road to be shoved up once again into ridges in the middle and on either side until the next storm. Rocking around inside the cabin, I noticed the dunes here were full of familiar three-cornered pippies, bleached white in the sun, sticking up out of the sand among the trees.

'These must be the middens,' I told Duke. 'They're thousands of years old.'

'Tens of thousands,' he corrected. 'Makes you think, doesn't it?'

The vegetation was thick all around us. God knew how it supported itself in the sand. Coast banksias with their distinctive yellow brushlike flowers blossomed among Moreton Bay ash, casuarinas and black wattle, the twisted roots of which the Aboriginals used for their boomerangs. A multitude of low bushes grew along the road, geebungs with their bright yellow flowers, the white-starred sand-berry bush, the pink blossoms of the boronias. Native orchids crouched low on the sand and everywhere the fascinating bright green foxtail fern hung its soft clumps which turned to red in the sun, looking and feeling just like a fox's brush. Blueberry ash flaunted its bright blue berries and prickly heath grabbed every space it could. Every now and then tall wedding bushes draped their veils of white flowers over the road, brushing against the vehicle as we jolted past.

A thought occurred to me and I turned to Duke. 'What was all that at the police station, about them hiding the Rover? Why wouldn't they have hidden it?'

Duke looked pained. 'Some bloody detective you are,' he said caustically. 'Figure it out, old son. Everybody knew the Rover hit Brent Eversleigh, there were dozens of eye-witnesses. Why hide it? Why not just leave it on the road outside town somewhere? There wasn't any need to stick it away under branches because there wasn't any doubt. Get it?'

I wasn't sure. 'But . . .' I began. My companion groaned impatiently.

'Look, Micky, if you'd wanted to have a go at Brent and then claim your vehicle was nicked, you'd make damned sure you put it where it could be found and leave some sort of evidence in it to show someone else had used it. Like a shred of cloth which wasn't yours, or the wrong brand of cigarette butt. You'd hardly bury it deep in the bush. You'd want it up front; there'd be no need to hide it.'

He wrestled the four-wheel-drive through a deep soft patch and scowled, concentrating fiercely on the track ahead. I subsided and watched the scenery.

Scribbly gums were everywhere, their white trunks patterned in scribbles by borers. Useles for timber, these gums, being so susceptible to termites. Dark vertical lines showed where the termite runs were, their great nests hanging in the branches or high on the trunks. Sometimes, I'd been told, a tree, completely eaten out, would come crashing down.

'Although I don't know how any trees grow here,' I commented after a while. 'There's absolutely no soil.'

Duke grinned, his humour restored. 'There are some nutrients, from the mulch of all the dead vegetation and insects,' he said, 'but only in the top eighteen inches or so of sand. The trees simply spread their roots out around them instead of straight down. The root spread can be at least twice the height of the trees. It's the only thing keeping them upright.'

'Bloody hell!' I felt distinctly uncomfortable.

'Cheer up, mate, they don't often fall over.'

As we drove, small Eastern yellow robins, resting in the middle of the road, flew up at our approach or flitted suddenly across the path in front of us to disappear into the bush with bright golden flashes of their back and tail feathers. We were climbing steadily into the huge dune system. In some places the track was covered with woodchips to bind the sand. We were now in tall, open forest, hung with vines.

Another vehicle approached and Duke pulled over. We scraped by, exchanging waves. We were driving under towering brush-box eucalypts, whose flowers give the pale, sweet-scented brush-box honey. Here, too, were the black-butts, the main commercial timber. We passed the odd tallow wood and I marvelled at the size of these giants, standing 150 feet high. A sign noted that one was 800 years old and I began calculating what that meant in terms of history.

'When that tree was a seedling,' I mused aloud, 'it was the Middle Ages. The Crusades were taking place in Europe, Genghis Khan was leading his hordes across Asia into Russia, St Francis of Assisi was forming his brotherhood.'

'Not much tallow wood left now,' Duke said prosaically. 'Wonder how that one escaped. It was over-logged years ago. It's an oily wood, perfect for outdoor steps, verandahs, you name it! My dad had an old truck with a tallow-wood body. And all the squash court floors in Australia are made out of it, it comes up so smooth and slippery.'

The road branched and was signposted. We took the fork to Lake Currawong and finally came out of the forest by the side of a beautiful, vast body of water, high in the dunes. Bloodwoods with their rusty bark, tall Brisbane wattles and melaleukas, the famous paperbark trees, grew down to the white beach which fringed the sparkling blue lake. A reed-bed rippled gently as the wind tide lapped the beach. Tents were scattered among the trees.

We pulled up and Duke turned off the engine. It was suddenly blissfully quiet, only the warning chuckle of a kookaburra breaking the silence. In the far distance, a fish-ing kite dropped like a stone to the water and rose swiftly, soaring against the green hills. The lake was easily a mile wide. I stepped cautiously down and swore, as once again the island poured into my shoes.

CHAPTER 22

As I shook the sand from my old joggers the sound of labouring engines revving and slowing drifted to us on the light breeze and three vehicles appeared along the track, pulling up beside us to disgorge Grant, two of his followers and the film crew. I went to Annie and helped her down from the high Range-Rover.

'What on earth are you doing here?' she asked. 'I thought you went off to Eversleigh with Duke.'

'I did. Annie, I have to talk to you—tell you what I'm doing. I know you won't like it, but . . .'

She smiled suddenly and put her hand on my arm. 'Micky, it's all right, I know already. The boss told us he'd asked you to work with Duke. You're right, I hate it, but —but it's what you're good at and you enjoy it, don't you?'

I started to protest but she covered my mouth with her other hand. 'Don't perjure yourself. I've always known you get—I don't know—satisfaction, I suppose, from finding out the truth. I'm afraid for you, Micky, but if it's what you want to do, I'll go along with it.'

My eyes searched her face and read how much it cost her to say it. I put my arm around her.

'Oh, Annie, I love you so much—and don't worry about me. I can take care of myself.'

Her eyes widened with astonishment as I echoed her familiar cry, then she began to laugh and hugged me. I was on top of the world until Jansen appeared at her elbow.

'It is a good joke?'

'The best!' I told him. 'Come to film Grant's Greenies?'

'We have today been down into the rainforest,' he said, his gaze flicking from me to Annie and back. 'It is most beautiful.'

I saw Duke and Grant in earnest conversation and knew

he was filling the MICO chief in on our meeting with Deakin and Hall. Grant looked distressed and nodded quickly several times. I knew he'd have a decent solicitor up by morning and breathed a little easier. I turned my attention back to the crew standing by the lake's edge with the couple I'd met at the hotel; Sally and the gipsy-man, whose name I'd discovered was Timothy. Jansen's camera was whirring, filming the chattering group. Damien White looked much more in keeping with his TV image after having been jolted and jerked across the island and subjected to miles of rainforest.

Sally was talking about the forest, the desperate need for its preservation, that a total ban on logging was the only way.

'They can't all be right, can they?' I whispered to Annie. 'I mean, all the different groups. They all have their own ideas. Well, who is right, then?'

She looked troubled. 'I don't know. Wish I did, though.'

I grinned. 'Wouldn't do you any good, love. Who'd listen?'

She slid her hand into mine. It was cold and trembled slightly. I squeezed it reassuringly and her eyes searched my face, then she looked away, seemingly absorbed by the filming. After a moment she said, 'We've had a threatening letter. The boss told us. Someone put it under his door. Saying we might be hurt unless we speak against the logging.'

'I know, he showed it to me. Why do you think I'm working with Duke?'

'We talked it over. We can't give in to threats. Inspector Reeves thinks it may just be an opportunist taking advantage of Melody's death.' She gave a little sob. 'How could anybody be so cruel?'

'On the other hand, it may well be some conservationist who's deadly serious. I'm taking no risks, love, and neither should you.'

'Inspector Reeves warned us to take extra care. He can't

assign police to watch us all, of course. I—I'm not worried, really; well, perhaps a bit.'

'How are the others taking it?'

'Oh, Paddy's mad as a hornet. He's really got his Irish up. He says be damned to them and we'll say what we want. Craig's as calm as always—takes it as part of the job. Hank's pretty angry. I think mostly for me.' She gave me a quick look. I didn't comment. 'The boss is concerned but determined to keep working if we all want to. You can't let people blackmail you. We're committed to telling a fair, unbiased story.'

'What about Peta?'

Her face clouded. 'Peta agrees with us. You don't have to worry yourself about her. She's not really one of the crew.'

'I'm worried about all of you. I wish to hell you'd call the film off, but I know you won't. I just hope there'll be no trouble tonight.'

It was late afternoon when we returned to the village and I was heartily tired of being thrown around the cabin. Apologizing to my kidneys, I thankfully abandoned the vehicle and left Duke to deliver it back to Mrs Robinson, while I headed for the pub. I needed a drink. The rest of the crew had gone back to the resort and I promised to join them later for dinner.

Once more I sat in the comfortable lounge with David Reeves, guiltily explaining my activities. He looked me over in silence and I came to a faltering stop.

'I can't keep you out of it, can I?' he said at last. 'All right, Micky, keep me informed of anything—I mean *anything*— of significance. I don't mind an extra pair of eyes and ears, but you watch yourself. I can't give you protection and now there's this threatening letter to take into account.'

'Don't worry, I'll be careful. What about those poor kids in gaol?'

'I'll make the necessary inquiries. I'll be seeing them myself tomorrow and I'll put a stop to all this nonsense from the sergeant. I know his type and I'll deal with him.

'By the way,' he continued, 'Hall and your friend Duke were right about the Rover. And I'll tell you this for free. The police searched the road where it was found on Monday. They can't think how they missed it. Of course, it was off the road and camouflaged, so it might have been there all along. The men were spread pretty thin by necessity. All the same . . .'

He fell silent as the barmaid came up, smiling at me. 'Here we are again. What'll it be, gentlemen?'

We gave our order and watched the room filling with much the same crowd as before. Once again, Wade and the Murchisons arrived and took the same table. Samantha Murchison seemed in high spirits, laughing and toasting her companions. Another win in the business world? I wondered idly.

The girl came back with the drinks. She looked quickly towards the bar and frowned as a loud voice called out, 'Come on, Max, ya thievin' bastard, set 'em up—on me, mate!'

'Problems?' I asked, and she flushed slightly.

'Johnnie Lowe,' she said with a gesture towards the private bar. 'Throwing his money around again, spending like there's no tomorrow, the silly sod.'

I saw the tears sparkling in her eyes. 'Sit down, love,' I said gently. 'Tell me what's wrong.'

She allowed me to persuade her and rubbed her eyes with the back of her hand, sniffing slightly.

'Look, love—I don't know your name . . .'

'Sharlene,' she supplied. 'Sharlene Smith.'

'Sharlene—why does it bother you what Lowe does?'

She looked at me helplessly. 'We're—sort of—going together,' she said, 'or we were, I'm not so sure now. I don't know what's got into him. Success gone to his stupid head, I reckon. He was OK—pretty reliable, bit of a wild streak, but he's young yet. Had the ferry and the charters. Then he gets real big ideas out of the blue. Took on a couple of extra blokes, bought a new boat—God knows how he was going to pay off the loan. Then suddenly he's got money coming out of his ears and he's getting drunk every night, just chucking it away—keeps telling me there's more where that came from and he'll end up a rich man.'

David shifted in his chair. 'But he's very busy, isn't he? He seems to be fully booked for weeks with the charters.'

'Yeah, but that's just his dumb luck. It's happened because of the trouble with the Greenies. See, that made all the extra people come up and then even more tourists, because Mitchell got in the news all the time.'

David leaned forward. 'And you're saying he expanded before that?'

She nodded miserably. 'Yeah, months ago. And now he thinks he's the bloody ant's pants. But what's going to happen when all this is over, eh? Where's the business coming from then?'

'What does he say?' I asked curiously.

She sniffed. 'Oh, he's the real big man, isn't he! Says not to worry my head about it and he knows what he's doing. But I reckon he's not that interested in me or the business any more. He stood me up on Monday night. We were going to have dinner and see a flick. It's my night off. So I waited and waited and he never came. Never even phoned. Wouldn't tell me where he'd been. And,' she continued, now thoroughly wound up, 'he nearly lost a charter on Saturday. Supposed to take a party out at ten-thirty but he didn't get out until over an hour later. Well, that sort of thing's going to get around and who'll want to hire him then?'

'Did he say why he was late?' David asked.

She shrugged. 'Oh yeah, he's always got an excuse, that one. Doing a job for Mr Wade, he said. But just because Mr Wade's important, Johnnie shouldn't let his other customers down.' She stopped abruptly as Adam Wade rose and left the lounge, passing close to our table.

The barman appeared from the public bar, looking harassed.

'Sharlene, I'm not paying you to socialize with the cops,' he yelled. 'Get in here!'

'Coming, Max!' She got up quickly and smiled at me. 'Thanks for listening,' she told me. 'It's not your problem, but thanks anyway, Mr Douglas. You're real nice.'

The ferry captain's voice rose above the hubbub next door. 'I'll be back, you blokes. Just going for a pee.'

David turned his glass slowly, watching the lights reflected in the amber liquid. Then he suddenly pushed back his chair and rose quickly. 'Come on, Micky!' I followed him out of the room and into the adjoining corridor, to the door of the Men's. As we entered, making casual conversation for appearance's sake, Adam Wade pushed past us, his face dark with anger, and slammed the door behind him. David raised a silent eyebrow. In the washroom Lowe was leaning against the wall, flushed and in a half-cut condition, fumbling with his belt. He hailed us indistinctly.

'Buy y'a drink, mates?' he offered unsteadily. 'Night's still a pup. Come back to the bar with Johnnie 'n' forget your troubles.' He suddenly broke into song, rendering a shaky 'Pack Up Your Troubles in Your Old Kit Bag' for our benefit. '. . . and smile, smile, smile,' he wavered and ground to a confused halt.

'That bloke looked as if he had troubles.' David jerked a thumb towards the door. Lowe chuckled and swayed where he stood.

'Silly—bloody—berk. Bloody mill—mill—rich man, he is, got stacks of the bloody stuff. So he loses a few bucks. Plenty more where that came from, eh! Gotta pay yer way in this world. Pay yer bloody dues, mate. But what's the use of worrying?' he sang to us. 'Smile, smile, sm . . . hey, you blokes not singing?'

'Not right now, Johnnie,' David said. 'How come Mr Wade's lost some money?'

'Ah!' He looked suddenly knowing and after a couple of false starts managed to tap the side of his nose with one off-course finger. 'Tha—tha's for some —' he lurched against David, who fielded him nicely and propped him back against the wall—'some to know and some to find out, eh!' He belched and sang at the top of his voice, '*Donald, where's your troosers?*' then laughed uproariously. 'Poor s—stupid sod, caught with his bloody pants down,' he hiccuped, then staggered to the door and went out calling, 'Set 'em up, Max, Johnnie's on his way.'

CHAPTER 23

David drove me back to Paradise Palms. Everyone was on the beach which was lit with barbecue torches. Coloured fairy lights twinkled and shone in the branches of the casuarinas on the dunes. Tables covered with banana leaves and hibiscus flowers bore up stoically under the weight of great platters of food; roast meat, jacket potatoes, salads and fruit. Most of the guests had costumes from muu-muus to grass skirts and everyone wore a frangipani lei. The staff in bright sarongs moved among the guests, serving food and drinks, and a trio played steel guitars and sang island songs. Sue Murray caught sight of me. 'Oh, good, you're in time for dinner. I was just about to put something aside for you. Now, it's just salad and veggies, and fruit?'

It was. Being a vegetarian is my small contribution to the rainforests of the world which are being bulldozed with frightening speed to make room for beef production. As Sue put my meal together, I made up my mind.

'Sue, I need to talk with you. It's important. Is there somewhere . . .'

'Of course. Come over here away from the others and we'll eat together.'

We spread a blanket under the trees and sat side by side in the gathering dusk, watching the bright, happy scene on the beach. I wondered how on earth to broach the subject of the letter when she gave me an opening.

'Mr White has told me you're investigating Miss Scott's death at his request.' She smiled. 'He's asked for our full cooperation. Is that what you wanted to see me about?'

'Yes, but this is personal, so I won't blame you for not telling me,' I said nervously. 'It's just that I couldn't help noticing how friendly you were with Sinclair Faraday.'

She was still smiling, thank God! 'We have an—understanding—to use an old-fashioned term.'

I took a breath and plunged in. 'He received a letter on Friday which shook him up quite a bit. I wondered if he told you what it was about.'

'I see.' The smile faded.

'Look, if it's nothing to do with this . . .'

'Is he in trouble?' she cut in anxiously. 'I haven't seen him today. He was supposed to come for dinner. He's got a temper, I know, but it's been very much exacerbated by all this publicity and the criticisms about how he manages the forest. I was worried that he might have done something stupid.'

'Not that I know of,' I said hastily. 'Look, love, forget the letter. I'm sure it's nothing. Probably personal. I'm sorry I asked.'

She faced me squarely, not listening. 'Micky, I'm afraid,' she blurted out. 'Sinclair's behaving oddly, he's like a time-bomb just waiting to go off. It's too much, all this stress. I know about the wretched letter and why it upset him, but if I tell you it'll put him in a very bad light. He didn't attack Brent, I promise you. They were very much in agreement over their work until recently. Sinclair's job is to manage the forests and select and mark the trees to be logged. Then Brent hires a contract logger to cut the trees and bring them to the mill. They're on the same side and they're friends. Very good friends. I don't believe Sinclair could have done anything to hurt Brent, in spite of—' She stopped and shoved her knuckles in her mouth.

'In spite of—what, Sue?' I prompted.

She brought her hand slowly down. 'I'd better tell you,' she said in a strained voice. 'I just don't know what Sinclair might have done, if you want the truth. The letter was from Brent Eversleigh. He said he had certain information that someone was deliberately stirring up trouble between Grant's people and the loggers and that this—person—had organized the bomb which nearly killed Hugh. He was so

horrified that he said he'd decided to support the World
Heritage Listing even if it meant the closure of the mill,
because what he'd discovered had shocked him so much he
felt he had to stop it at all costs. He told Sinclair he was
going to Brisbane on Saturday to be interviewed by Damien
White and he'd expose the whole story. He invited Sinclair
to meet him on Friday afternoon and he'd explain everything.' She stopped and bit her lip. 'That's all.'

My heart was thumping. 'And did he go to see
Eversleigh?' I asked her.

'Yes, he went to his office at five o'clock. Brent wanted
him to know before he left the next morning for Brisbane.
He knew he'd be picking up his mail as soon as he arrived
on Friday afternoon.'

'I see.' I put my arm around her drooping shoulders.
'It's all right, Sue. If he didn't do anything he's got nothing
to worry about. But I think you should encourage him to
tell Inspector Reeves everything.'

'He won't. I already tried. He just lost his temper. What
on earth . . . !' Her head jerked up as the sounds of furious
exchange broke on our ears. 'Oh no!'

I followed her as she ran towards the voices. On the path
to the beach Faraday and Grant were confronting each
other. Faraday looked murderous, Grant's eyes flashed
behind their thick lenses.

'What d'you mean, telling White we knock down everything and burn it?' Faraday was yelling. 'You know bloody
well that it's not left like that. If you knew a damn thing
about the forests you're so keen on protecting, you'd know
if we didn't, the trees wouldn't regenerate. Blackbutt needs
fire to reproduce, or didn't anyone tell you the simple fact
that some seeds are only triggered by fire?'

'Oh yes, blackbutt,' Grant shot back. 'And what about
the rest? You're promoting one species at the expense of
the others because that's your bread and butter. You'd see
all the other trees destroyed for a blackbutt monoculture.'

'Balls! Look, we've got records back to nineteen-fifty that

say we've kept the same percentage of species that always existed. And that's after logging.'

'Forty years!' Grant exploded. 'And Mitchell's been here for forty thousand years! You don't care about the ecology of the island. You're just farming timber for your own purposes!'

'Shit, you're a blind bastard! No wonder you can't see without your bloody glasses. I'm a professional and I've got my reputation on the line here. D'you think I'd clear the trees if I didn't know there was a young forest coming up again? D'you know what numbers we've replanted this year already? D'you know how many old trees we leave? And yet you make out we log the lot!'

Sue gave a distressed cry and ran between them. 'Oh! Please, please, stop it! Everyone will hear you. Sinclair, Hugh, you're acting like children, fighting over something you both love.' She burst into tears and both men, suddenly shocked, patted her awkwardly.

'Oh, Sue, don't, I'm sorry.' Faraday led her back to the house.

I glared at Grant. 'You blokes fight over the darnedest things. Why can't you all get together and agree on how to save the island? It's beautiful!'

He shook his head in disbelief and left me standing there.

CHAPTER 24

I crossed to Eversleigh with the film crew. Duke was going over with Hugh Grant. My heart sank as we arrived at the island jetty and I recognized Greenies and loggers alike crowding into their rocking craft. This meeting was supposed to be for the Eversleigh townsfolk to put their point across. I could see it becoming a free for all.

There was quite an armada of little boats speeding across the channel, their foaming wakes gleaming white under a clear sky blazing with stars. I looked up with awe. We city dwellers made a poor bargain when we swapped the glory of the night sky for neon.

The Town Hall was in Arthur Street at the opposite end to the jetty. We decided to walk and fell in with the various small groups from the island who had made the same choice. The streets for several blocks around the Hall were lined with cars squeezed bumper to bumper. As we drew closer to our destination we could hear voices raised and the rhythm of chanted slogans.

'What do we want?'

'No more logging!'

'When do we want it?'

'NOW!'

I noticed several TV vans parked outside the main entrance and their crews were circling the milling crowd, recording the action. Placards were waved and a scuffle broke out, to be quickly suppressed. Hugh Grant was exhorting his people to demonstrate peacefully. Jansen had brought his kit along and quickly set it up, hoisting the camera to his shoulder to begin filming. Paddy stayed with him as the rest of us made our slow way into the hall, jostled by the crush of Eversleigh's citizens. It bothered me to be so surrounded by people possibly hostile to White. The ecologist was easily identifiable and several people were looking at him in recognition—his famous face was a dead giveaway. I was relieved to see a handful of uniformed police in evidence. Annie looked pale but I couldn't push my way past a pair of over-large ladies to get to her. I finally caught her up as we found seats towards the back and as we sat down I put my arm around her. Beside her, Peta was looking wide-eyed and a little apprehensive.

I glanced around the hall at the women of Eversleigh in their short-sleeved print dresses, their men in shirtsleeves. I saw Adam Wade and the Murchisons at the front in the seats reserved for VIPs. Samantha Murchison stuck out like an orchid in a field of daisies. I noticed several ladies looking her way with envy. Duke was close by them. Typical of him to wangle one of the best seats. Our friendly newsagent was present with his wife, a thin, meek-faced woman, and near them was the postmistress in a flood of conversation with someone in the row behind her. The room was filled with the buzz of chatter, sounding overloud to my anxious ears. The police positioned themselves around the walls.

The stage had been draped with bunting and on the back wall a large photograph of a young Queen Elizabeth smiled down at the crowd. A long table with half a dozen chairs faced the audience and a microphone screeched and whined as a harassed technician adjusted it. The TV channel and radio stations had clustered their own heavily padded microphones around the table and their sound engineers were crouched in a group on the floor below the stage.

'Why aren't you down there?' I hissed at Edgely.

'Ah!' He smiled urbanely. 'Mr Grant has arranged for us to receive a copy of one of the recordings. I felt I should be back here with Mr White and the girls.'

And Paddy's watching Jansen, I thought. That's nice, but it wouldn't stop any serious attempt. Hell! I cast a glance over my shoulder. Jansen and Paddy were with a small knot of people standing at the back of the hall, waiting for the show to start. I drew a shocked breath. Beside the big Dutchman was an even taller figure. I half rose, then sat down, feeling like an idiot. The man was here to watch over Wade. He wasn't even looking at the men beside him. All the same, I'd be on my guard. Annie looked an inquiry and I shook my head in answer.

The noise hushed as a group of men walked on to the stage and, after a hurried consultation, arranged themselves at the table. The centre chair was occupied by a small, plump man in a dark suit. His hair was greying blond and he had a round, placid face. I recognized him from various TV news reports. Albert Kline, Eversleigh's mayor. He tapped the microphone and spoke loudly into it.

'Can you all hear me, down at the back? Right, then I'll open the meeting. I've been asked to chair this discussion. I know you've all got questions you want answered and you'll all have your chance. If you've something to say, don't shout, just raise your hand. We've got a couple of roving mikes in the audience, so please wait until one is passed to you. Now, I'm not going to say much as you all know the problem and I want the ministers to have as much time with you as possible.'

He introduced the group at the table. The Government ministers for Industry, Employment and the Environment were present as well as Sinclair Faraday and Tom Eversleigh. I looked with interest at the mill-owner. He was tall and his domed head was completely bald, which he balanced with a long silver beard and fierce, bushy eyebrows. He looked biblical. Any moment he'd raise his staff and the crowd would part . . .

The audience applauded politely if unenthusiastically as the Environment minister got to his feet.

'My Government has a responsibility to all Queensland,' he started. Brave lad, I told him silently. 'However, until the Inquiry has submitted its findings we are not prepared to speculate on the future of Mitchell Island. The Inquiry has heard some very convincing arguments from both sides.

However —' he cleared his throat as a mutter arose—'one of our election promises was to increase National parks and wilderness areas and to save greater tracts of native forest —and we will honour that promise.'

Voices from the audience begant to be raised. The mayor held up his hand. 'Please hear the minister out. You'll have your say later.'

'We have to make these decisions based on the suitability of the area, the wilderness value balanced with the need for employment, industry and, of course, economic viability. These choices are never easy ones. We're looking at a multiple of factors and no decision has been made or will be made until we have the recommendations of the Inquiry. However —' he paused again on his favourite word, then continued carefully—'my personal opinion, for what it's worth, and I stress that it is just a personal opinion, is that Mitchell Island is an ideal site for preservation, that the economic problems Eversleigh would face could be overcome by bringing in other industries to the town, and I think you're going to have to get used to the idea of an eventual cessation of logging.'

Angry cries from the body of the hall caused the mayor to intervene again. The minister raised his voice above the protesters. 'I think this meeting will accomplish more if we come from a realistic base and begin to look at ways we can soften the impact for Eversleigh's citizens. We're here to listen to you but I don't want to give a false impression.'

He sat down and hands shot up around the room. Albert Kline pointed to a man.

'Yes, Bob, wait until you get the mike, mate.'

'Don't bloody need it!' The man's voice easily drowned out the hubbub. 'I'm here to represent the farmers, Al. We've built up our properties for generations. You stop the logging and our livelihood's up the bloody spout. We supply the town with all its fresh produce, veggies, milk, we built up the cheese factory, Eversleigh buys our meat—what are we supposed to leave our kids? And their kids?'

The newsagent leaped up and plunged in, his face getting redder by the minute, angrily shaking off his wife's pleading hand.

'What about the small businesses?' he yelled. 'You close the mill, we're all done for. It'll be the end of Eversleigh. We need the logging and no bastard from the city's going to take it off us!'

'All right, let's have some order.' Kline was on his feet again. 'Shut up, Jack, and sit down. We don't want a free for all. The chair recognizes Les Brown.'

'The logger,' Annie mouthed at me. He stood up, a big man, and waited for the microphone. When it arrived he spoke in a slow, North Queensland drawl.

'Jack and Bob are right, Al. We've built Eversleigh and my blokes all live here. We've brought up our families here. A lot of us have kids leaving school soon. What are we going to tell them? Sorry, kid, but that lifetime job you thought you had just got ripped off you? Sinclair'll tell you. Properly managed, the timber'll last forever on Mitchell. We use sustainable yield. Looking at the island now, you can't tell which areas were logged a few years ago. The sites have all regenerated and I reckon none of you could pick the difference. Look, if a forest's logged, it's still a forest, right? It's produced some timber and of course some logs have been removed but it's still a forest. We don't knock it down and leave it there.'

A voice called from the back, 'What about the changes you make? It's not the same after you blokes have been there.'

Les Brown nodded. 'Sure, there'll be some changes. You've got some logs taken out. But, with good management, it should be possible to log a forest permanently.'

'That's a con!' the angry voice behind me yelled. 'You go after blackbutt, you clear fell a football field at a time, then you go in with chainsaws and knock down everything else—the forest oaks, bloodwoods, the understory—then you put a bloody fire through it!'

This was the argument that had set Sinclair off during dinner. Now he spoke from the stage, his calm manner a surprising contrast to the way I'd seen him, squaring up to Grant.

'I agree it doesn't look very nice, but if we didn't do that we'd create an unnatural mix of species. The fire opens up the canopy and lets the light in for the young, newly planted trees and the understory grows back. That's how nature does it. We just duplicate nature.'

Tom Eversleigh leaned forward and spoke clearly across the yell of derision from the back.

'I don't know how many of you conservationists realize that the Forestry Department was started because of the concern of a miller seeing the timber being totally cut out. He pressured the Government to protect it. I agree, they were pretty ignorant back then and weren't that successful at regeneration, but nowadays Forestry blokes like Sinclair are highly skilled and trained. We only harvest any area every twenty or thirty years and we replant and look after the forest. You blokes all know me. I bloody well love Mitchell.' His voice choked with emotion. The mayor patted him on the shoulder.

'Thanks, Tom. We know you're under a lot of strain with young Brent. We appreciate you turning up tonight.'

The Minister for Employment stood up. 'We don't want to be involved in a another debate for and against logging,' he said. 'We're concerned with what the future holds for Eversleigh. And it does have a future, believe me. We're planning very substantial compensation amounting to several millions and the Federal Government's guaranteed to back us dollar for dollar. We don't necessarily see this as handouts to individuals but to be used for the good of the whole community for job retraining and similar ideas. My colleague here —' he indicated the Industry minister—'has a scheme to bring in more industry, especially tourism and projects like your cheese factory, including a small cannery for locally grown produce to be marketed in Asian countries. The small businesses won't suffer. We'll create more jobs in the long term than you'll lose.'

The Industry minister nodded. 'Absolutely,' he agreed. 'There's a scheme to buy a large area of land to plant quick-growing trees suitable for woodchips. In five years we could have a fully operational woodchip mill fed by its own plantation.'

Someone yelled, 'Five years is a long time to go hungry, mate! What are we supposed to do until then?'

More hands were raised, more questions fired, complaints made, anger and frustration expressed. But after a while the voices began to drop and people murmured to each other. There were more fierce accusations from the Green lobby at the back of the hall but Faraday was keeping himself well in hand and refused to be drawn. Several times his face looked stormy, but the man had more self-control than I'd have believed possible.

CHAPTER 25

In the end, after all the impassioned arguments, I thought most of the people at the meeting recognized the writing on the wall and were prepared, if ungraciously, to accept the inevitable. The dissenting voices were fewer and the meeting broke up at 9.30. We started to make our way out through the crowd. Several shouts of 'Why didn't you say anything, Mr White?' and 'Damien White's on the side of the loggers' were raised but White just smiled gently and stopped to talk to this one and that and they were quickly silenced.

Outside, the leaving crowds were met with a very organized Green protest. We'd heard the muffled chants throughout the meeting and had realized we'd have to run the gauntlet. I put an arm around each of the girls and began to edge them away from the crowd. The Wade/Murchison clan appeared with their tame giant in tow. I realized unhappily that the protesters had been busy. They'd spent their time tying green ribbons to the aerials and door handles of every car in sight. The Town Hall porch was festooned in green. Angry howls came from the more vocal drivers and a shouting match began.

I saw the now furious newsagent tear the ribbons from his car and rip them apart. He wrenched open the door and flung himself on to the seat, revving the motor loudly. Before anyone could move he suddenly drove at the Greenies who dropped their placards and scattered. Women screamed, men grabbed for wives and children. Craig Edgely had been speaking to Hugh Grant who'd remained outside with his supporters and the car went straight for them. At the same time, a terrified child ran across the space which had magically cleared, screaming for her mother.

There was a cry of anguish from behind me and an enormous man hurled himself in front of the car. The driver, suddenly realizing the enormity of his action, slammed on the brakes and the car slewed to a screeching halt. Almost under its wheels, the huge minder held the child, soothing her, a look of horror on his face.

There was a shocked pause and then people were swarming around. The police helped the newsagent out of the car. He looked near to collapse. His frightened wife hurried to his side. People surrounded the giant rescuer, slapping him on the back, applauding him. The child's mother darted over and, too dazed to speak, snatched up her daughter, tears running down her face. I heard the minder's deep voice, 'Yeah, I'm OK. I got kids in my family—my sister's girls.'

I shook my head. Perhaps there was more to the man than I'd appreciated, but I sure as hell wasn't going to make it top priority to find out.

Craig Edgely was white and spluttering with indignation, his cool calm finally deserting him.

'Did you see?' he stuttered. 'That madman tried to kill me. He bloody tried to kill me. *Me!*'

Jansen and Paddy had joined us. Jansen grinned. 'No, not kill you, Craig. Just to scare Hugh, I think.'

'Well, it amounts to the same bloody thing. I could have been killed! *Me!*'

Duke pushed his way to us. 'My stars! Anyone hurt? Great! Micky, I'm on my way back to Mitchell. I'll pick you up in the morning.'

The beach party was still in full swing when we arrived back at the resort. As we drew closer Sue appeared, running, calling out to me.

'Micky, hurry. It's Mr Jordan on the phone for you, urgent.'

I ran with her, stumbling through the sand. Duke's voice, taut with anger, came down the line.

'Micky, I've just had a call from Fran. They've got Maria!'

'What!'

'She's been kidnapped, snatched from the house. They left a note saying if I went to the police she'd be killed.'

'But, Duke, you have to tell the police . . .'

'Shut it, mate!' he said curtly. 'No police, do you hear me? They've given me an ultimatum to stop the investigation, or else. If I lay off, we'll get Maria back safe. Fran's going crazy.'

A hundred things to say raced through my mind. All I could manage was, 'Hell! How did it happen?'

'Fran had the doors and windows open. It's a hot night down there. The bastards must have been watching the house. They knew where Maria's room was. Must have seen Fran putting her to bed. Fran was in the kitchen, heard a noise and went to see. A couple of men were in the hall with Maria. She was half asleep—just woke up and started screaming. The men had stocking masks. Fran couldn't recognize them. They had a gun but she went for them anyway, like the little beauty she is. They knocked her down.' His voice was icy. 'She's OK but it took her a minute to get up and she didn't see them drive off. Just heard the bastards. They told her if she went to the police she'd never see Maria again. They'd left a note on Bambina's bed. I'm going back to Brisbane tonight to be with Fran. Micky, you're on your own. I can't do anything. I'm not about to risk my kid's neck.' His voice shook. 'Don't tell Reeves, do you hear me? We can't afford it. You have to do this yourself. Follow Faraday up and find out about Wilson and anything to do with Austral. Report back to me at home.'

'What about Grant? He's here now.'

'Tell him nothing! Just get on, mate. You know as much as I do. Find out what's going on. We've got to get Maria back safe.'

I stood for a long time after he'd hung up, the receiver still in my hand, my dazed thoughts chasing each other around desperately. It meant one thing. Somehow we'd got very close to the truth, although I didn't know what it was yet. But if I just went over our every move, every conversation, it had to be there.

I went back to the bungalow and sat in the dark, thinking. The luau partied on. I badly needed to talk to someone and I needed an ally. I reviewed the available candidates. Who was strong enough, wild enough, stupid enough to join me in a spot of madness? And reliable. Someone I could trust with my life.

Ten minutes later I went back to the beach. The film crew members were beginning to leave the action. Another busy day ahead. The big Dutchman had been seeing Annie to her cabin, the creep. He sauntered past me, walking light on the cloying sand, and gave me an amused look.

'Jansen!'

He stopped, surprised. I had to look up at him, something that doesn't often happen.

'Ja, Douglas?'

'I want to talk to you—privately. Somewhere quiet. I—er—want your help.'

CHAPTER 26

I'd stopped talking. Jansen had listened with hardly a word
—just the occasional query. Now he pushed his chair back
and studied me, an odd gleam in his eyes, his smile crooked.

'Answer me one thing, Douglas. Why me?'

I shrugged. 'Anyone who's stupid enough to lie down
and let an elephant run over him has to have some staying
power.'

His grin broadened. 'Maybe Faraday is not so brainy as
an elephant.'

I slapped my hand on the table. We were in the dining-
room, otherwise deserted. 'Look, are you in or out?'

His brows lifted slightly. 'You are jumpy. That's not so
good. You need a cool head for this.'

I was silent. He was right, damn him. My nerves were
shot to pieces. I was twitching at the slightest noise. He
continued to watch me coolly.

'This alters nothing between us—with Annie.'

'No, I'll still get her away from you!'

'Oh, ja? Good luck!'

'Well?' I asked impatiently.

His slow smile embraced me. 'Ja, I'm in!'

Surprisingly, I felt a whole lot better. He leaned towards
me, lowering his voice. 'Now, your case against this wild
man, Faraday, goes like this. Tell me if I miss anything.
He comes to Eversleigh on Friday afternoon, picks up his
mail at four o'clock and gets a letter which infuriates him.
In a mood of great anger he goes to see his friend Brent
Eversleigh who tells him that he no longer supports the
cause of logging and is about to denounce a person who
has been causing all the trouble and has tried to kill Hugh
Grant. Faraday next appears at the Colonial Hotel saying
he must stay the night as he has missed the ferry. But

there is a special six o'clock service on Friday nights which presumably, unless his meeting with Eversleigh was a very long one, he would have had ample time to catch. The next morning he breakfasts in a very worried state, looking "like death", according to the waitress, sitting by a window with a full view of the jetty. So he is easily able to see Hall and Deakin drive up and leave their vehicle. He then steals the Land-Rover, waits for his former friend and ally and runs him down.'

'He could have. The waitress said he was so quiet at lunch she couldn't get a word out of him. A man in a state of shock after an impulsive, desperate action. Duke said he was on a very short fuse. Sue's opinion was that he was a time-bomb waiting to explode. You yourself called him dangerous on Tuesday night.'

Jansen grinned. 'I said he looked *bloody* dangerous. Man is an animal, ja? In spite of all he pretends to be so superior, he shows the same reactions. I know animals very well, Douglas. Especially wild, nervous animals. Frightened animals. This is your Sinclair Faraday. A worried man may panic and do a stupid thing—you saw the incident tonight —but you are forgetting one detail in your story.'

'And that is?'

'That is, there were many witnesses who, although only one saw clearly, all were sure that there were two people, a man and a woman, with long hair, the man bearded. Sinclair Faraday does not have a beard, neither is he two people.'

I thought about it. 'He could have persuaded a woman,' I said slowly, 'I'm sure of it. The locals are very sympathetic towards him and equally antagonistic towards those they see as his persecutors. Sue Murray was very convincing earlier, but they're lovers. He might have persuaded her to help him, then assure me he was innocent.'

'Was Sue in town on Saturday morning?'

'It'd be easy enough to find out.'

'All right, it may be as you say, Douglas, but what about

the description? Sue has long hair, but it is fair, not brown.'

'They might have worn disguises.' I sounded unconvincing even to me.

'Then that would mean premeditation and how could Faraday know that two people with the exact same description would leave their vehicle within his reach at the convenient time? Was he working with Hall and Deakin, members of MICO? No, this was not premeditated. This was an impulse, it must have been. And Faraday fits the character of a man who would act on such a wild impulse —but how did he do it?'

'I don't know,' I admitted, 'but I'll swear it was him.'

'Then we'd better prove it. The forestry camp, it is not so far from here. We could easily visit it and look around.'

'Look around?' I was puzzled.

'You are too nice in your mind, Douglas. Search his place, of course. If there is any evidence, it must be found.'

I felt profoundly uncomfortable but I couldn't see what else we could do. If we confronted Faraday with our suspicions he'd laugh in our faces—or shoot us on the spot, but he'd obviously deny everything.

'Tomorrow. I'll talk to the boss. They can do other things instead of filming. We get some sleep now and an early breakfast, then off we go. The foresters' camp will be deserted if we are lucky.'

'Look.' I felt awkward. 'You don't have to take the risk. I—I could do it myself. I shouldn't be involving you in anything illegal.'

The smile lifted the corner of his mouth, his eyes were clear and glowing. 'You couldn't stop me,' he said simply. 'This I will enjoy more than you, I think. And besides, there is Maria, who must be a very frightened little one. I do not approve of this sort of thing. Whoever is responsible, we will find him and he will pay for it.'

The door opened and Sue came in, smiling at us. 'Are you staying here all night? Would you like a coffee?'

'Good God, is that the time?' My watch said midnight. 'No, thanks, Sue, I'm for bed.'

'We were talking about the trouble here.' Jansen's deep voice was slow, smooth, his eyes watching her. 'And the sad accident to Mr Eversleigh—or attempted murder, I should say. Many people were in town on Saturday morning?'

'Yes, it's always busy. And there were a couple of spring sales at the dress shops.'

'Ah —' he grinned—'always with the ladies, the clothes. I suppose you were there as well, looking for some bargains.'

She laughed. 'Well, yes, actually I was. I like to rummage in the sales. And I'm always needing nice clothes, being the manager here.'

'You didn't see the incident, though?'

'No, thank goodness!' She looked grave. 'I'm deeply relieved I was nowhere near the station.'

Something she'd said caught my attention.

'Are you just the manager, Sue? I thought you owned the resort.'

She shook her head. 'I used to, but some months ago I was doing badly and needed extra finance. I'd approached the banks for a loan when, out of the blue, Adam Wade offered to buy me out and give me a permanent job as manager—everything I had before but without all the worry. I accepted, Paradise Palms belongs to Adam, now.'

A little bell rang in my mind. I should have listened, but even if I had, I couldn't have stopped what happened next. It was already too late.

CHAPTER 27

Al Wang has this theory about dreams. He says that as you go through the day you only consciously observe so much, but actually you record everything else, subconsciously. Every sound, every gesture, every expression, all the little background details you don't know you've noticed. Then, if anything's out of line, you work it out in your dreams in some sort of dramatic symbology that's guaranteed to get your attention. If you want to know what your dreams mean, he says, have a look back over the last twenty-four hours and see what made you feel uncomfortable—or what you forgot to notice.

So it wasn't surprising that I woke up in a cold sweat, saving myself in the nick of time from being crushed to death by a whole lot of shop window dummies in pioneer costumes, all of whom were laughing and screaming and screeching . . .

'Oh, the divil! Them blasted birds again!' The mound that was Paddy pulled a pillow over its head and snorted.

Jansen was standing by my bed in the grey dawn light. 'You are awake!' he said softly. 'Good! I will see Damien and then we will eat.'

I slipped out of bed and dressed quickly, then stepped into the raucous morning. The sea air was fresh and cool, the lemon sky was paling rapidly into pastel blue, and bird songs filled every available space not already shattered by the cockatoos. A soft whistling overhead made me look up to see a flock of rainbow lorikeets among the gum blossoms over our cabin.

Annie was awake. I didn't know whether to be glad or sorry but I knew I had to tell her what was happening. She looked at me accusingly.

'You've no business dragging Hank into this,' she said

angrily. 'It's bad enough with you and Duke. What on earth made you ask Hank?'

'Duke had to go back to Brisbane—an emergency,' I improvised. If I'd told her the truth she'd have insisted on my going to the police and she'd not listen to any excuses. 'It's all right, love. We're just going to see some people and —er—ask a few questions.'

'You're lying!' she shot back. 'Don't ever try to play poker, Micky, you'd be a dead loss!'

'Love, I can't tell you everything,' I said in despair. 'Please trust me. Jansen and I will look out for each other. I just didn't want us both to disappear without you knowing.'

Her mouth was tight, uncompromising. 'Right, now I know. So you can run along and play your stupid games and get yourselves killed for all I care!'

'Oh, darling Annie.' I pulled her into my arms and tried to hold her but she fought furiously to get away and turned her back on me.

'Just—just *go!* And good riddance to both of you!'

I knew she was crying and stood helplessly, until she stormed into the bathroom and slammed the door. She ignored my anxious pleading so I had no choice but to leave her, my heart heavy.

Jansen gave me no sympathy. 'You should not have told her,' he said briefly. 'Don't talk to me about honesty. Time enough to worry her to death when we return. Then we could show her we were safe. Now she'll be concerned for us all day.'

None of the film people had arrived for breakfast by the time we left at six o'clock. We borrowed one of the resort's four-wheel-drives and Jansen steered us up into the interior. The foresters' camp was deserted when we arrived. It was set in a thickly timbered valley beside a freshwater lake. This water was shallow and stained a clear red/brown from the tannin in the tea trees which stood around it. Unlike the parched lakes in the high dunes, which were fed by streams and rainwater, this was connected to the water table below and would rise and fall with the water-level.

I slid cautiously down, eyes watching for any movement. A large goanna froze on a tree-trunk, its head turning slightly to watch us, and a pair of bright green parrots, startled, flew swiftly across the lake, scolding crossly in harsh whistles. The long-drawn-out crack of a whip bird sounded in the forest but everything else was quiet. The air was still cool, with the sweet, distinctive smell of the Australian bush.

The camp was scrupulously neat, settling into its environment with a natural harmony. It consisted of half a dozen small timber huts, a communal shower block and a long building with a shady verandah which housed displays and specimens for the tourists. Faraday's hut was larger than the others and had a small office attached. His name was on the door, which was locked.

'No matter!' Jansen said and prowled noiselessly around the back. After a moment he called softly. I found him by an open window, a disapproving look on his face.

'Careless!' he said, shaking his head. 'To go out and lock the door so carefully but to forget to close the window.'

I looked at him suspiciously, not in the least gulled by his innocent face. As big as he was, he went through the window like a cat. I made it less gracefully and reluctantly followed his cool example as he quickly began to open drawers and search, neatly, methodically. He'd have made a great burglar. Although I couldn't stand the man, I had to admire his courage.

I found the letter in a desk drawer in Faraday's office. It followed pretty closely the story Sue had told me and named no names.

'Could Faraday have been the one who's stirring up trouble and who sent that bomb?' I mused. Jansen looked up from a diary which he was reading with impunity.

'Why would he want to do a thing like that?' he asked with a quick frown. 'If there is too much trouble, the Government will find a third solution, isn't that the theory?

Against the loggers *and* the World Heritage listing. Faraday wants the logging to continue. He might try to stop Brent Eversleigh but would he make trouble for his own side? No, Douglas, not to my way of thinking.'

An envelope was pushed to the back of the drawer and hidden under files and folders of statistics. I pulled it out.

'I wonder what this is all about,' I said, puzzled. Jansen glanced at the company name on the envelope.

'What is Austral Development?'

'It's the local Real Estate Agency.' I took out the single typed sheet with the company letterhead.

'What is it?' Jansen came to look over my shoulder.

'Well, I don't know,' I said slowly. 'It looks like a list of company directors. And how the hell is Future Property Development involved?'

I stared at the details of the three companies listed. The penny was slow to drop but when it did it exploded in my brain.

'Bloody hell!'

Jansen started. 'Keep it down, Douglas! What have you found?'

I was shaking. 'Jansen, we've got to get out of here. Before anyone finds us. We'll take this. The Inspector will be very interested. It's not Faraday. I've been on the wrong track all along!'

'Who is it, then? You don't explain.'

'Later!' I told him over my shoulder. 'And for God's sake, lock this bloody window again!'

I read the list aloud to him as he drove carefully, negotiating the rough track. The jerking about made my eyes woozy but I gave him the gist of it so he'd understand.

'Wilson Properties is owned by Austral Development. Duke found that out. This confirms it. Bernie Wilson is also on the board of directors of Austral. However, Austral also has a parent company, Future Property Development. You see their signs everywhere, "For Your Future". Well, guess who's on the board of Future Property Development?'

'Bernie Wilson!' he said promptly.

'And someone else,' I told him grimly. 'The managing director. Adam Wade.'

'Now that *is* interesting.'

'It's more than interesting. It's bloody suspicious. When Grant took on the Government over the Mitchell land sale, the company involved was Wilson-Nishida, as in Bernie Wilson. Now we discover that Adam Wade, who already owns property here, is the managing director of the parent company of Austral which owns Wilson Properties.'

'Grounds for suspicion, ja, but no proof.'

'Well, add this! Two months *after* the case had been lost and Wilson and Nishida had gone their separate ways, Wade, through a special law created so Dan Nishida could buy a piece of beach in North Queensland, just happened to quietly slip through his own sale and bought the beach front at his place.'

Give him his due, Jansen wasn't slow. 'So you think he was still hoping to buy the land? That he hadn't given up after the court case was lost?'

'Looks like that, doesn't it? And we're looking for someone who wants the loggers *and* the Greenies out and the Government so fed up it might take a soft option.'

'Go on.'

'Right. Now a few months ago, before all this trouble started, two things happened. Wade bought out Sue at Paradise Palms, and Johnnie Lowe, who often works for Wade and seems to know a thing or two about him, suddenly expanded his business. Although he had no extra clients at that stage, he took on two other men and bought a new boat. Unless the man's psychic, he must have had some knowledge that he was about to get a lot of work.'

'Like now, with all the trouble attracting extra people?'

'Like in the future when there's a five-star resort operating and he's got an exclusive contract!' I said bitterly. 'But why would Wade choose him? He's a drinker, loudmouth, half flash and half foolish—what we Aussies call a bit of a lair and a bit of a drongo.'

'Maybe he could be bought,' Jansen suggested. 'Persuaded to look the other way over shady deals. And, of course, he has the ferry service and the charters already.'

'We've got to see him,' I decided. 'Let's get back to the village. The ferry will be in at ten-fifteen. We can ride over with it and talk to him.'

We made the trip in what must have been record time, although twice I was jolted high enough to hit my head on the cabin roof. I cursed Jansen, who just grinned and whistled a bright little tune. I thought we'd miss the ferry after all, and was thankful to see the jetty ahead but puzzled by the number of people and vehicles standing about. I easily picked out David's red thatch, head and shoulders above the rest, and immediately felt guilty, then caught myself up, annoyed. He couldn't possibly know I was keeping Maria's kidnapping from him and I'd promised Duke. I tried to concentrate on our reason for being there.

'Lowe's late getting away.' I eyed the ferry. 'And he's not loaded up yet. 'It's twenty-five past ten.'

As we left the vehicle, Sharlene ran up to me, her eyes bright with tears.

'Have you heard?' she asked breathlessly. 'Johnnie's disappeared. He stayed on Mitchell last night and should have taken the ferry over at nine-thirty this morning for the first run, but he hasn't been seen. There's a line-up of people on the mainland all doing their blocks and we've been trying to get one of his men to come over and pick up the ferry and get it back. He's on his way now from Eversleigh.'

'Have the police done anything?'

'They've been all over the ferry. Johnnie sleeps on board. But there's not a sign of him.'

She gulped and her voice broke. 'They—they think—he was pretty drunk last night. They think he might have come back here, lost his footing and fallen into the water. The channel's deep and the currents are bad. If—if he did, he'd have been swept out, around the Head—maybe—maybe out to sea.' The tears ran down her face. 'They've got a search party out now, combing the beach. He could've been washed on to the surf side. Oh God, poor Johnnie!'

CHAPTER 28

Jansen and I took the weeping Sharlene back to the hotel and left her with an anxious Max. Then we sat in our four-wheel-drive and looked at each other, both thinking hard.

'An accident?' I said at last. 'Last time I saw Lowe he was drunk out of his mind and had just had a heated argument with Adam Wade.'

'Ja? Tell me.'

I recounted the scene in the Men's the night before.

'Mr Wade comes into this story too many times for my liking,' he said thoughtfully. 'I wonder if he was the one who attacked Mr Eversleigh.'

'Same argument that you put up.' I objected. 'He doesn't have long hair or a beard and he's only one man. He couldn't have known Hall and Deakin would arrive so conveniently while he was having breakfast . . .' I stopped and stared at him, my brain suddenly shocked.

'What is it, Douglas? Don't clam up on me now.'

'Wade has the only other table with the same view over the jetty and he was at the Colonial Hotel for breakfast on Saturday morning. Bloody hell! And he went to see Eversleigh earlier that morning. He was seen entering the Mill office at eight-fifteen by Sharlene who was waiting for the dress shop down the road to open. He left just before eight-thirty and went to the pub to meet his niece and nephew. Of course, once again, Samantha Murchison does not have long hair, neither does her husband wear a beard.'

'They are the same age, though. And a couple, man and woman . . .'

'Did you *see* the Murchisons last night? She's a yuppie, smart from her bobbed hair to her Gucci shoes. No one would take her for a hippy, not even on the smallest glance. He's the same, not a hair out of place. He and Wade dress like real outdoors types, courtesy Cardin, but I'll bet it's all image. They wouldn't get their manicures all mucky, and—oh hell! Oh bloody hell!'

Suddenly I knew! Ignoring Jansen's demands to be told what was going on, I flew out of the vehicle and ran the few yards to the Mitchell Hotel. There was a red phone in the entrance and I was quickly through to the waitress at the Colonial.

'Tell me,' I demanded urgently, 'the day the displays were vandalized. Was it Saturday?'

'Why, yes.' She was surprised. 'How did you know?'

'I'm psychic,' I said shortly. 'Just after breakfast, wasn't it?'

'Right again! What else do you see in your crystal ball?'

'I'm prepared to bet I can tell you exactly what the damage was!'

I was right again. Three in a row isn't bad! Then I asked some questions I should have thought of earlier.

'It was the display next to Wade's table,' I told Jansen. 'I'd noticed one of the dummies wore a modern, short wig. It looked out of place. And the male was the only one without a full pioneer beard. The short wig was only temporary, until they could replace it with another like the one that was stolen. And two napkins were ripped up and thrown in a corner. Two *green* napkins!'

'Green headbands.' Jansen nodded.

'Spur of the moment, like you said. Wade and the Murchisons are three of a kind and Samantha works for him—or did. Try this. Brent tells Wade he knows what he's up to and he's going to Brisbane to spill the beans. They were mates, so he'd be bound to tell him first, maybe even see if he could make Wade stop. Wade meets the Murchisons and tells them the predicament. Then, with perfect timing, although only for some, Deakin and Hall arrive and, in full view of three very worried people, leave their vehicle for the taking. One of the trio looks at the dummies with long wigs and beards, so similar to the Greenies, and realizes that, with practically no effort or risk, they can pose as the unfortunate pair and solve their problems in one hit, no pun intended.'

'Then they concealed the vehicle, removed the false hair and joined Wade?'

'Not quite. Here's an extra piece of news. They didn't leave the pub together. Wade had another cup of coffee and read the paper. The Murchisons went out—in a hurry—because Samantha had, quote, suddenly remembered the dress sales, unquote. That was about nine-fifteen. She came back, by herself, just before ten with no shopping-bags—but she *might* have left them in their vehicle outside, if you can believe Mrs Murchison would shop for clothes in Eversleigh at all. *He* arrived, out of breath and agitated, about ten minutes later and the three of them left. The damaged display was discovered just after.'

Jansen was watching me intently. I took a deep breath and continued.

'Now, that looks like Donald was left to abandon the vehicle and, instead of simply wiping off their prints and leaving it on the road somewhere for the police to find, he decided to hide it. In the words of Harry Andrews, he's a "bit of a dill" and probably thought he was concealing evidence or something. Sharlene said they'd been in the Mitchell pub on Sunday afternoon, having a hell of a row, Wade and his niece "having a go" at Donald for something. They'd probably just found out what he'd done.'

'What, that he'd left it covered with branches in the bush?'

I frowned. 'He couldn't have, then. He wouldn't have had time to take it out of town, conceal it, and walk back. They must have done that later, *after* the police had searched that area. They were pretty safe, you know. No one would connect the yuppie Murchisons with Hall and Deakin. They're well known here—and Wade seems gener-

ally liked. They'd simply take their luxury launch and come
over to Mitchell—Bob's your uncle!'

'How are you going to prove it?'

I felt decidedly sick. I'd just remembered Samantha
Murchison's performance the night before, very pleased
with herself, toasting the others. Duke's inquiries about the
beach sale and the Austral-Wilson connection must have
frightened Wade and his relatives, enough to make them
shut him up any way they could. Had I been looking at a
lady who'd just successfully engineered the kidnapping of
my god-daughter?

'We'll have to go to Wade's,' Jansen said grimly, scaring
me to death.

'My God!' I yelped. 'Do you know what's up there?' I
told him. He looked unimpressed. 'Try to lie down and let
that gorilla run over the top of you, you berk!' I fumed.
'He'd kill you without a thought!'

'Douglas, I should tell you, I am very hard to kill.' He
didn't know what he was up against, ignorance being
bloody bliss! He looked amused. 'There's a road that takes
you above the Fisherman's Head. If it's not possible to
approach from the beach, we'll observe from above and
when the coast is clear, see if we can get any evidence to
support your theory.'

Oh, fine, I thought bitterly. How come I keep getting
involved with bloody heroes!

Some time later Jansen drove us off the road, into a small
side track; an old logging road, now closed. We were on a
ridge overlooking the Head, with a breathtaking view of the
passage, restless cobalt flecked with white, and the mainland, with Eversleigh shimmering in the hot noon sun.

'We can't see Wade's place very well from here,' I said
softly, 'the trees are in the way.'

Jansen pointed to a lower ridge, to our left. 'There's a
small shack down there and it looks as if it has an un-
obstructed view. Let's climb down and see if anyone is at
home.'

We got down, sliding through the sand, holding the trunks for support. The little shack, perched on the ridge, was thrown together haphazardly from timber, corrugated iron sheets, palm frond matting and fibro. There was a rough stable door, the lower half shut, but no sound of inhabitants. A familiar scent was in the air, at once sharp and mellow, with a faintly nutty overtone.

'We'll risk it!' Jansen whispered and, noiseless as a leopard after prey, approached the open door. I mimicked his example, one careful foot after the other, silent as breathing. When the twig under my foot snapped it went off like a pistol shot, frightening me out of my wits. I yelped.

Suddenly there was pandemonium! The door flew open and a giant was towering over us, his shotgun levelled, his wolf's grin horrible. From inside a woman's voice, querulous, called, 'No, Tiny, wait!' I yelled and grabbed Jansen.

'Oh, shit! That's him!' Without waiting, I pulled the Dutchman back and, to my horror, felt the sand give way under my feet. As the shotgun exploded we fell back, crashing and sliding down the ridge, bushes breaking as we smashed into them, me in a state of total panic, Jansen swearing and cursing me for a fool. We came at last to a slithering halt and lay motionless, breathing heavily. Someone was whimpering. I realized it was me and shut up.

We sat up cautiously and looked at each other. Jansen was a mess! Sand and leaves in his hair, a twig in his beard, his shirt ripped open. His face was bleeding. He looked me over, the slow, lopsided grin spreading.

'You're a sight!' he said, then began to laugh. It was infectious. I began to smile, then I was laughing with him, howling with relief. When the gale of mirth subsided, he held out his hand and said, 'Hank!'

I gripped it, grinning. 'Micky!' I told him.

We picked the bush out of our clothes and hair, un-sanded our shoes and pockets and reviewed our position.

'You know, Micky, when a man is bitten by a wild animal, he as two choices,' Hank said thoughtfully. 'He can be afraid for the rest of his life, or he can go back and face the animal.'

My mouth dropped open. 'The animal has a shotgun!' I reminded him.

'And a woman. I wonder what they were doing. There was a strange scent around the shack. Did you recognize it?'

I tested the air in my memory. 'Turpentine?' I ventured. 'And—and linseed oil!'

'I thought so, too. Well, do we face your wild animal, or run away?'

I looked up the slope. It was a hell of a climb. I sighed and began to pull myself up.

CHAPTER 29

We sat in the little shack drinking tea, looking around the small room. The smell of turps and oil was strong and the walls were stacked with canvases of every size, boxes of oil paints, brushes, rags and all the artist's paraphernalia. On an easel by the door was a painting of breathtaking beauty. White beach and shadowy green bush, mysterious, inviting you to push further in. The woman working deftly at the easel was dressed casually in a skirt to her ankles and a man's shirt knotted at the waist. Her long white hair was tied loosely back with a scarf, her old, lined face made extraordinary by a pair of bright blue eyes, full of youth and sparkling with interest. A collection of small charcoal sketches lay on the only table at which a huge man sat, cleaning brushes.

'You're Old Maggie,' I said, 'otherwise known as Margaret Yates.'

She twinkled at me. 'That's right, dear. This is my hide-away, and you're the first to find me. I'm hoping you won't tell anyone, because it's a quiet, beautiful spot and I'd be very sad to leave.'

'You won't have to leave, Maggie,' Tiny growled. 'I'll keep people away.'

'Like you do for Mr Wade?' I asked caustically.

He chuckled deep inside him. 'That's right. Worked for you, didn't it?'

'It's all bluff,' Margaret laughed. 'Tiny wouldn't hurt a fly. People see his size and think he's dangerous but he's a lamb.'

'You shouldn't give your lamb a shotgun,' I told her sourly.

'Oh, now, never you mind. He only loosed it off over your heads. He wasn't going to shoot you, just scare you away. He looks after me, see, and I'm teaching him how to paint. He's getting very good. Does lovely bird studies. As soon as he's got the money he's going to art school in Brisbane, aren't you, Tiny?'

He looked sheepish and shuffled his feet.

'Now, gentlemen, if you're over your fright, you'd better tell me what you're doing, prowling around my home.'

Hank was loving my embarrassment.

'We were trying to find a way down to Adam Wade's— er—without Tiny stopping us,' I floundered. 'We—er— wanted to have a look around.'

'It must be your day for trespassing.' She smiled at my discomfort. 'Suppose you tell me why?'

'We're looking for something,' I hedged. 'I'm—er— doing a spot of investigating for Damien White—because of the death of one of his crew.'

'The Scott girl,' she said at once. 'Yes, I heard all about that in the village. There's not much happens on Mitchell that Old Maggie doesn't hear about. Now, that Adam Wade,' she continued warningly, 'he's no good, do you hear me? I don't trust that man. I can read people pretty well, you know. And Tiny agrees with me. That's why he's leaving.'

The big man nodded. 'He's up to something all right, him and that Johnnie Lowe. Johnnie's been up to the house, demanding to see Mr Wade, like he's got some right to be there. Up to all sorts late at night, though I dunno what.'

'Like when, late at night?' I asked curiously. He thought back, frowning.

'Saturday night, it was. Mr M. had Johnnie take him fishing. That's a good one! That's not what they were up to. Mr Wade didn't like it, whatever it was. He had a meeting that night, at Eversleigh, and I went with him. When we got back, real late it was, Mrs M. told me to go to my room and stop there or I'd be sacked. I could hear Mr Wade and the Murchisons making a hell of a racket arguing with each other, pacing about. They were still at each other next day. Then, Monday night, Mr Wade had Johnnie carting stuff over to the mainland all hours. Ferry came into Mr Wade's jetty near ten o'clock. I dunno what for.' His deep voice was scornful. 'They don't trust anyone, even me. I don't do anything illegal. I'll scare people away, that's my job —' I caught a twinkle in his eye and felt a complete fool—'but I wouldn't be in on anything that wasn't straight up. I was told to get lost again and not to show my face or else. It was no skin off my nose. They must have had a load of stuff because they drove it down to the barge. Then they came back to the house and had another shouting match. Sounded real worried. Then, in the morning, you wouldn't believe it, but Mr M.'s burning rubbish in the incinerator. Says he's decided to tidy up the yard. Him!' Tiny snorted with derision. 'He never did a day's work in his life, not real work. All he knows about is ripping off investors on the Stock Exchange, that's his idea of work. I dunno! I'll be glad to be shut of that lot. I wouldn't let them look after any kid of mine!'

'What's Adam up to, do you know?' Margaret broke in eagerly. 'You *do* know, don't you?'

My giveaway face! 'I've a good idea of some and can guess at the rest,' I said. 'Is Mr Wade at the house now, Tiny?'

He shook his head. 'No, went down to the village. Someone rang and said Lowe's gone missing and the police wanted to talk to Mr Wade. They were seen together last night having some sort of barney.'

'Is there an easier way to the house?'

He showed his teeth. 'Track out the back, take you straight there. I'll come too. OK, Maggie?'

'Don't any of you dare to not come back and tell me *everything!*' she called after us as we followed Tiny out of the shack.

As we approached the pink stone house I suddenly clutched Tiny's powerful arm.

'What about the Murchisons?'

He grinned down at me. 'Don't worry, mate. They've gone, too. Off on their own business.'

My heart slowed to something near normal and we made our way through the lush, tropical gardens.

'It's *soil!*' I realized aloud. 'Genuine, honest-to-God, firm soil.'

'Mr Wade had truckloads of it shipped in so he could grow things,' Tiny said scornfully. 'It's not natural. Island shouldn't be mucked with.'

I sighed. Another Greenie. I wondered whose particular side he was on.

'Where's this incinerator?' Hank asked, *sotto voce*.

'Around the back. I'll show you.'

It was brick and steel, a solid job. Hank squatted down. 'Has it been lit since Tuesday morning?'

'No, Mr M. used it last.'

Hank began to scrape out the ashes with his hands. I saw it first. A small pink blob, distorted by fire but still attached to a scrap of pink wool. It rolled out with the rest.

'A pearl button,' I said and couldn't say any more. Hank took it gently from my fingers.

'Poor Melody,' he said, and his voice was very deep.

'What's that?' Tiny was pointing. It looked like a heap of matted fur, or hair. Like a . . .

'This is it, Micky.' Hank held it up. 'It was pushed to the side and didn't burn properly. He must have been in a hurry. I'd say this is the remains of the wig and beard.'

The voice behind us was cold.

'I'd say you're right, whoever you are. Get your hands up!'

She'd crept up as quietly as Hank on the prowl. I wondered if my whole day was going to consist of looking into shotguns.

Samantha Murchison was ice-cold and briskly efficient. No one argued. She had a look which let us know she'd not hesitate to pull the trigger. Probably enjoy it.

We were joined by Donald Murchison. 'Well done, darling. Good thing we decided to come back early.'

Samantha marched us into the house. Donald fumbled over tying us to the chairs in the living-room but got it right after a few goes. Like Tiny said, not good at the practical stuff. She'd have been quicker, but she seemed to prefer holding the gun.

'All right,' she snapped when Donald stepped back at last. 'Now just who are you?'

I looked back at her. I was in so deep now and for sure I wouldn't live through it, so I finally lost my temper with enthusiasm.

'You can call me Micky,' I told her cheerfully, 'and why don't I find something nasty to call you?'

Her eyes flashed. 'I could shoot you for trespass, my friend. Don't tempt me.'

'Only we were with Tiny, who is employed, may I remind you, by your uncle. Hardly trespass.'

'Don't take us for amateurs,' she said contemptuously. 'You came up here with a shotgun, killed Tiny, my uncle's guard, and attacked me. I managed to reach the gun and defend myself.'

I gave her what I hoped was a superior smile. 'Nice one, Sam, only I'm a friend of Inspector Reeves. He knows why I'm here. Try another story.'

She looked furious. Not used to being argued with, probably. Now I know what they mean when they talk of speaking through clenched teeth.

'Just who the hell *are* you?'

'Language!' I reproved. Hank stifled a laugh, the lunatic. Here he was, facing death and enjoying it!

'I'm someone who's been finding out about you,' I said blithely. 'About you and Wade and Johnnie Lowe and the Wilson/Austral/Future connection. And about you using the nicked Land-Rover to hit Brent Eversleigh. You shouldn't have let Don dispose of it. He's not bright enough. I bet he drove it straight back to Adam Wade's private

lock-up across the passage. Who'd think of asking a local
big shot to open his garage? Who'd imagine the friendly,
retired Mr Millionaire Wade would be involved? Then he
got Johnnie Lowe to bring it across to Mitchell on Saturday
night, under cover of a fishing trip. Very unlikely. You were
furious because you knew it would look sussy when the
police couldn't find the Rover. So you got Johnnie to take
it back on Monday night, but then you had to make it look
as if it had been hidden there all along. You knew the police
had searched everywhere. Must have been very worrying.
Silly old Don!'

'You can't know all that!'

'Well, I know that Donald hired Lowe for a so-called
fishing trip on Saturday night, and paid him handsomely,
also that Lowe had a date on Monday night with Sharlene
at the pub, but stood her up because he had a job to do for
Mr Wade. Come to think of it, Lowe practically told me
that Donald had been caught with his pants down.'

'That little turd!' Donald Murchison exploded angrily,
and was silenced by a laser look from his wife.

'Shut up, you idiot. Go on, Douglas.'

I went on. 'I know Damien White was on the beach on
Monday smoking his pipe and saw a boat he described as
a ferry passing the resort—a bit out of its usual route,
wouldn't you say?'

She laughed but it sounded strained. 'You seem to know
it all.'

'Probably not all, although I reckon one of you is responsible for Lowe's disappearance.'

Hank turned his head to look at me. 'How do you know
that?'

'Well, think about it, Hank. Johnnie Lowe couldn't have
seen the accident clearly. He ran out of the newsagent's
and was standing near the window, not the kerb. The footpath was crowded. Lowe's only five six or so. He couldn't
have seen over everyone's heads. He didn't come forward
until after he'd done the ferry run, and later he held up a

charter for an hour doing a job for Wade. Well, the only thing he was doing at that time was telling the police he suddenly remembered he saw the whole thing and could positively ID the two suspects. That was the job he was doing for Wade. Wade must have met him at the ferry and told him exactly what to say. Probably paid him well, too. He must have done well out of the family, by the money he was suddenly flashing around.'

'Why would they kill him, if he was so useful to them?'

'Ah, that's it, isn't it, Sam?'

She stamped her foot. 'Don't call me that!'

'Temper, temper, Sam!' I grinned at her fury. 'Oh no, don't shoot me until I tell Hank the best part.' I looked across at him. 'Johnnie thought he was on to a good thing. He'd been approached by Wade earlier. Something like, you do anything I ask and I'll make sure you get exclusive rights to service my new resort. But when it came to hiding the Land-Rover, Lowe realized he had enough on Wade to try a spot of blackmail! Isn't that right, Sam?'

Hank let out his breath slowly and nodded. 'Ah, of course. That would fit.'

'The money, the "more where that came from", the row with Wade and, now I come to think about it, I actually *saw* Wade leave the money in a newspaper at the Memorial Park—and Lowe picked it up! God, how stupid I was not to realize earlier. So one of you happy band followed Lowe back to the ferry, hit him on the head, was it? Pushed him overboard? He'd be no trouble, in that state. He was barely standing when I left and that was early. You could have done it yourself, Sam. Did you?'

I stopped abruptly. There was a noise somewhere in the house, high-pitched. A child was crying.

CHAPTER 30

Suddenly Tiny's words at the shack slammed back into my mind—I looked urgently across at him in time to catch his muscles straining, his biceps huge as footballs. He quickly relaxed.

'What did you mean, you wouldn't let them look after any kid of yours?' I yelled at him.

'It's their niece,' he grunted. 'They're looking after their niece.'

I stared in disbelief at the Murchisons, my anger reddening my vision. 'You bastards!' I swore and shouted, 'Maria, Maria, bambina, it's Micky!'

The cries stopped and there was a joyful scream. 'Micky, Micky! Come get me! I wan' Mama!'

'Patience, bambina, Micky's coming!' I managed to get the chair mobile, half standing, my helpless arms lashed to the back struts. As I lurched forward Samantha coolly lifted the gun and levelled it at my stomach. Then there was a sudden snapping noise and Tiny, free of his bonds, hurled himself at her. She swung around. The noise of the shot was deafening and Tiny staggered back, his good hand groping for his other shoulder, one arm hanging useless and spilling blood all over the carpet. He stood, staring at the red splashes, frozen for a millisecond with shock, then, with a roar of rage, he picked up his chair in one hand and hurled it across the room. Samantha went down with a scream. Tiny, unstoppable as a mad bull, swung around to Donald, who began to back away, several shades paler. He cast a quick look at the gun lying beside his motionless wife but thought better of it. When Tiny reached him, his face was livid with fear. One punch was all it took from that great fist. I heard a sickening crunch as his jaw gave way.

As Tiny began to untie us one-handed, still dripping on

the floor, there was an urgent hammering at the door. I let Hank deal with whatever it was. He was the hero. I was too busy searching the house for Maria. I found her, crouched by the door in a bedroom, black curls a mess, her face tear-stained. We hugged each other until David Reeves broke it up.

'Some old lady,' he explained. 'Old Maggie? A local artist. She rang us at the hotel and said you were in trouble.'

'She must have seen the Murchisons coming back as we were on our way down. Thank God for her!' I smiled tiredly. 'All I want to do is go back to the resort and maybe sleep for the rest of the day.'

'You're coming back to the hotel with us!' he said firmly. 'I want a statement from you. By the way, Lowe's body was washed ashore earlier, on the east side of the island. It could have been an accidental death but there's a suspicious abrasion on the back of his head which rather points to deliberate murder.'

Hours later Hank and I faced the rest of the crew who listened with shocked faces as we told our story.

'Melody was just unlucky,' I said gently. 'She chose the exact time for her walk when Johnnie Lowe was taking the Land-Rover back to the mainland. She saw it being driven down to the ferry and overheard the whole story. Donald Murchison was keeping watch and he knocked her out and drowned her in one of the salt-water pools. They had a heated argument about it and decided to take her inland to the nearest fresh water to divert attention from their area. Later they found her cardigan where it had fallen and when they were getting rid of the wig and beard, they burned the cardigan as well. They didn't bother to do a thorough job. After all, the rich Mr Wade was inviolate, they thought. And another fire would have been lit to burn rubbish in the next few days, taking care of any last traces.

'So the threat wasn't against the film crew,' I continued, with a vague idea of comforting them. 'It was just bad luck.'

I heard Al Wang's voice. *Micky, no one can die one second*

*before their time. Do not talk of accidental deaths to me, or prema-
ture deaths. A life of even one day is a complete life and all is
well.*

'That note under your door —' I looked at White. 'They
got Johnnie Lowe to put it there.'

White nodded slowly. 'Thank you, Micky. I believe we
all owe you a debt of gratitude. I feel somewhat distressed
that I was the cause of your getting into an extremely
dangerous situation. We would like you to stay on with us,
as our guest, of course, and allow us to show you a happier
time than you have had so far.'

I stood up. 'No, thanks, boss. I wouldn't mind having a
look at the rainforest, if I can stand another ride over these
bloody roads, but then I'm off. I can't take any more of this
island. The sand gets in everywhere!'

They dispersed to change for dinner. I followed Annie.
Hank put his hand on my shoulder.

'Micky, there's something I should tell you . . .'

'Later, mate! I've more important things to do.'

Outside, the beach was a setting for tropical passion;
curved palms, the scent of a thousand flowers, the whole
flooded by moonlight. Annie and I walked by the water,
saying nothing. Then she faced me.

'Micky, I—I did a lot of thinking today—with you and
Hank out there, facing heaven knew what danger. I thought
about us.'

I wanted to say, 'I love you,' but I didn't feel it was a
good time. Then she said it instead and got it all wrong.

'Micky, I love you, I really do. I think I always will. But
that love has changed. It wasn't anybody's fault. I think I
always knew I couldn't commit myself to a relationship
with you. You're a friend, my best friend, but that's not
the sort of love that's enough for a marriage. Not for me,
anyway.'

I nodded. I'm not always stupid. I saw the way she
looked at Hank when we got back. I could have killed the
bastard!

'It's not just that, either.' Her eyes searched my face anxiously, willing me to understand. 'I don't want to be confined to one place any more. My world is so much wider now, so much more exciting.'

'But you hate your men getting involved in danger,' I reminded her. 'Hank's a nutter! He sat there, a shotgun at his head—and laughed! He'll always be like that.'

'Just like you, in fact.' Annie smiled slightly. 'Talk about the pot and the kettle! But I've discovered something. I've grown up since I left you, Micky. Fran was right. If that's what Hank is, then I have to accept that part of him, too —or else it's like taking away the very essence of him. I'm sorry, Micky—and I'm so ashamed, too.'

'Ashamed? But why?'

Even in the moonlight I could see her flushing. 'You'll despise me when I tell you. I was so jealous of Peta. I thought you invited her, wanted her more than me. How stupid! Really childish! And you, you accepted Hank as a friend from the start and when you needed help, you turned to the one man you should have hated. You—you're much —finer than I am, Micky.'

I looked at her gravely. Don't judge me too harshly, but I wasn't about to shatter her illusions.

Hank was waiting for me at the bungalow, his face sombre. Paddy had already gone to the dining-room. I hesitated, then took his outstretched hand.

'Sorry, Micky, I tried to tell you. I asked her to marry me when we got back. She said yes.'

'She told me.'

'Friends, ja?'

I met his eyes and smiled in spite of myself. 'It was—it was a good thing you were there. Thanks—mate!'

'I'll take care of her.'

'I know you will. She won't thank you for it, though.'

His other hand gripped my shoulder and he rocked me back and forth a couple of times, taking space out of his happiness to share my grief. Then he let me go. 'Coming for dinner?'

'Not yet.' Eating was the last thing I needed. I couldn't face the bright lights, the chatter of the dining-room.

'Well, see you later, then.'

'Yeah, later, Hank!'

I walked back to the beach, heartsick, my emotions exhausted. The water lapped gently at my feet, a mopoke called somewhere near at hand. My mind was a blank, although I tried to find something to tell myself—that it was better to have loved and lost, that Life Goes On, we'd always be good friends. Eventually I managed to feel something and was vaguely surprised to discover it was hunger that was fighting its way to my attention.

The thought of facing Annie, Hank, the sympathy of the film crew, now almost certainly toasting the happy couple, brought a sinking feeling to my stomach. Fear's a funny thing.

When a man is bitten by a wild animal, I heard Hank say seriously, *he can be afraid for the rest of his life or he can go back and face the animal.*

I turned and made my way back to the house. I needed my dinner.

CHAPTER 31

There was a great difference in atmosphere, coming from the sunny dune tops with their tall, open forest to the rain-forest valleys. Here it was much cooler; danker, with only the odd splashes of sun flecking the sand tracks, which were damp with moisture. Fallen logs were thickly covered with mosses in a constant primæval ritual of decay and regeneration. It was quieter in this deep place, the only sounds the trickling of a fresh-water stream and the chink-chink of bell birds. The trees sported clumps of fungi and many giant trunks were buttressed. Strangler figs quietly expanded in a silent death struggle with their hosts. High above me stag and elkhorns adorned the branches, and the air smelled richly of decay.

I sat on a huge stump of satinay, perhaps three thousand years old. It could have easily seated a dozen in comfort. Tim and Sally had brought me here, and their voices had long since faded into the thick forest. Everyone was busy this morning since Sinclair Faraday had arrived at the resort looking dazed and given us the news that there was to be a moratorium on logging until Lionel Blake, QC, had heard all the submissions in his Inquiry and had made his decision. The Greenies were packing up camp. Faraday was being relocated, Tom Eversleigh was firing off angry letters to the Government, Eversleigh township was in shock.

I'd breakfasted early and gone to see Old Maggie. She'd not died from curiosity but reckoned it had been touch and go. She'd listened, entranced, applauding our dramatic rescue by Tiny, at present recovering in the Eversleigh hospital, endangering the two beds they'd had to put together to hold him. I'd farewelled the artist regretfully.

'I bought one of your charcoal sketches at the souvenir

shop,' I told her. 'I'll treasure it—and I'll never tell, I promise.' I grinned. 'A friend of mine is over the moon because she just bought a Margaret Yates from Fields' Gallery, but I'm perfectly happy to have a sketch by Old Maggie!'

Duke and Fran had arrived like a whirlwind just after dinner the previous evening, Duke's eloquent face a study as he snatched Maria up and hugged her with one arm, holding his other hand out to me, emotion robbing him of speech. Maria had almost fully recovered from her ordeal, having been crooned and fussed over first by Sharlene at the pub while Hank and I answered David's questions, then by Sue, Annie and Peta as they washed her, fed her and put her to bed until her parents arrived. She was inclined to be teary when she saw her mother but our concern had subsided when she'd informed Fran that she wanted to stay with all the nice signoras and eat yummy cake.

'They'd spoil you rotten,' Duke had told her, 'let's get you home, Bambina.'

Later, Peta had found me on the beach. Her eyes were dark in the night, her face glowing as the moon slipped between fast-moving clouds, her expression hard to fathom. When she spoke it wasn't the sympathy I'd dreaded, but of purely practical matters.

'You wanted to see the rainforest before you left,' she reminded me matter-of-factly. 'We'll be going up to Hugh's camp in the morning and you can go down with some of his people.'

'Not too early,' I warned her. 'I've got to see someone first thing. I owe her.'

'That'll be OK. They'll wait for you. And I've got to get back to my firm, so I'll be driving down to Brisbane tomorrow afternoon. If you're coming back as well, perhaps you'd like to come to my place for dinner—save you cooking a meal.'

I looked down at her in silence, feeling her friendly smile easing the ache in my heart, warming me . . .

'Sure, why not!' I said at last. 'Thanks, love, I'd enjoy that.'

I looked around at the thick green world which closed me in. The ground dropped steeply to the stream which was so clear the water was invisible, only the ripples in the sand bed showing its pristine path. A kingfisher dropped suddenly in a flash of iridescent blue feathers, and returned to its perch high above the stream. I'd been sitting still for so long it had given up worrying and was getting about its business. Growing in the water was the biggest fern I'd ever seen, easily ten feet across, the primitive King fern whose ancestors went back at least fifty million years. Tall picca-bean palms grew along the stream's edge. Tap them and they give a hollow sound. They used to be used for water pipes. Two-hundred-foot satinays reached up through the canopy, trunks twelve foot round. Lianas hung like in a Jungle Jim movie. I craned upwards to glimpse patches of sky so far above me I felt dwarfed by the sheer height and size of the rainforest. Everywhere was moss and fern and damp mysterious dark places. I felt a strange awe at the vast beauty of this cathedral world.

I slowly touched the great tree-stump, tracing the rings, feeling the rough bark, amazed at the variety of mosses vying for its destruction. I sighed. I would have liked to see a three-thousand-year-old tree. How mightily it must have stood here, towering into the distant sky, it and all its giant brothers.

When I moved the kingfisher flashed off downstream, startled to find I was still alive. I slowly returned to the track, brushing damp moss and bark from my jeans. I looked back just once, silently saying goodbye to the remains of the ancient satinay. Then I sighed, and began to walk back up the path to the MICO camp.

THE END